MURDER AT CHEROKEE POINT

Kendall Sheepman Company, Cheboygan, MI

ISBN: 978-0-9903104-1-9

Cover photo courtesy of Marta J. Olson

Design by HeatherLeeShaw.businesscatalyst.com

Printed in the United States of America

PETER MARABELL

MURDER AT CHEROKEE POINT

A MICHAEL RUSSO MYSTERY

Frances, ceci est pour vous

"In reality they all lived in a kind of hieroglyphic world, where the real thing was never said or done or even thought, but only represented by a set of arbitrary signs."

—Edith Wharton, *The Age of Innocence*

1

Kelsey Sheridan walked quietly down the gravel road. Not that he had to be quiet at two in the morning. A stiff wind came off Lake Michigan and curled around the dark ornate cottages of Cherokee Point Resort Association, reaching Kelsey on the road that ran behind the houses.

He'd walked this road all his life, so he didn't need the moonlight that moved in and out of the clouds to guide him. Kelsey glanced at the name signs at the end of each driveway. Abbott, Griswold, Buchanan. The patriarchy of the Association. These men, including his father, Roger Sheridan, ran the resort like a private kingdom. They made the rules, limited the membership and deemed privacy an inalienable right. To Kelsey it felt oppressive—not in a political sense, although it was, but in its reverence for tradition, its tenacity to keep everything the way it had always been, its fear of the locals in Harbor Springs and Petoskey.

Kelsey Sheridan wanted more from his life than to take over his father's manufacturing company and to assume the throne as an oligarch at Cherokee Point. He did not share their obsessive need for privacy. He'd followed in his father's footsteps to Dartmouth, but he wanted to make his mark as a novelist. And he did his best creative thinking late at night over by the tennis courts, smoking good weed and dreaming of being a successful writer of mysteries, his name recognized alongside those of Chandler, Hammett and Parker. Kelsey climbed into the umpire's chair, as he always did, pulled out a carefully rolled joint and struck a match. "Jesus!" he said, startled. The light illuminated the body of Carleton

Abbott, lying face down on the apron of the court, his left arm awkwardly caught in the tennis net. A dark stain matted the hair at the back of his head. The cloistered world of Cherokee Point had just blown apart.

> > > >

Little Traverse Bay on a warm June morning could make a guy want to play hooky. I leaned back in my chair and put my feet up on the desk. The window was open and an easy breeze brought fresh air into the office. Too bad I had to spend the whole afternoon in court. Too bad I had to earn a living on such a nice day.

"Michael," I heard Sandy say from the doorway. Sandra Jefferies runs the office and makes me a better lawyer. "Captain Fleener's here to see you."

"Come on in, Marty," I said. Martin Fleener was a Captain of Detectives with the Michigan State Police. A twenty-year veteran, he'd moved north in 2010, reassigned to the Petoskey post.

Marty walked into the office and dropped his six-foot, two hundred pound frame in the chair opposite my desk. His charcoal, double-breasted suit was set off by a red guards striped tie over a white shirt. Class.

"To what do I owe your visit on such a nice morning? Can't imagine you need a lawyer, but I see you brought something from Johan's," I said, pointing to the bag in his hand. "Want some coffee while we sample the baked goods?"

He nodded. "With a little milk," he said.

Sandy brought in two mugs of coffee and walked out with a cinnamon sugar donut. "Nice trade," she said.

Captain Fleener sipped his coffee. "You know, Michael, when I got here four years ago, I thought I'd miss Grand Rapids. Didn't happen," he said, shaking his head. "Surprised, I guess, how quickly I got to like it here. But every so often, I'd rather be in the city." He bit off a piece of glazed donut, sipped more coffee and put the mug on the corner of the desk.

"You looking for a transfer?" I said.

He shook his head. "Got a nasty one, Michael. Getting squeezed hard. You heard about Carleton Abbott, I assume?"

"I'll say. It's all anybody's talked about for a week. Can't go anywhere. The bar at Chandler's, even the checkout line at Home Depot, for crissake. Your case?"

He nodded. "Wish it weren't. Back in Grand Rapids, there'd be somebody else to throw it to. But here . . ." He shrugged.

"Never known you to want off a case," I said.

"Some noses out of joint," Fleener said, "and they're attached to some very powerful people who don't like cops prying into their private world."

"Talking about Cherokee Point?" I said. Fleener nodded. "Sorry if I sound naïve, but aren't you just doing your job? I mean, a guy gets killed, the cops are going to ask questions, right?"

"Sure thing," he said. "But some of the people who live out there don't think the rules apply to them. Don't think they should have to talk to us. Or the prosecutor. Hell, the guy at the gatehouse told me he's not supposed to let ambulances in the main entrance because the sight might upset the residents. How upset's a heart attack gonna make ya?"

"If you want to rant about the neighbors, how about I buy you a beer after work?"

"Actually, Michael, this is business." Fleener took a drink of coffee. "We want you to help us out."

"Who's 'we,' Marty?"

"Me and Don Hendricks." Don Hendricks is the Emmet County prosecutor. "Now, Michael," Fleener said, raising his mug in the air. "I know what you're thinking."

"You do?"

"Look, we're getting a lot of pressure. Don and me. The folks at Cherokee Point say they understand we have a job to do, but that's where the cooperation ends. Don't ask questions. Don't bother the residents.

Don't snoop around the property. I introduce myself and people turn around and walk away. I'm not investigating a murder to them, I'm prying into their lives. I'm an inconvenience."

"What is it you think I can do?"

"You know the Point, right?" I nodded. "And you have clients out there? Some friends, too? So they don't regard you as an alien from another planet."

"But if I ask questions, what makes you think I won't get the same treatment?"

"Because you're a familiar face. They know you professionally, sure, but they know you socially, too." Fleener shifted in the chair. He looked annoyed, but not at me. "They'll talk to you because you're not an intruder. Tell 'em you're helping to keep us away. Tell 'em whatever you want. Damn it, Michael, we gotta a dead body with a bullet in the back of the head. But I also got a senator from Indiana out there, a congressman from West Michigan and one ex-governor. And all of them have called Hendricks."

"You don't mean to tell me those people are trying to stop your investigation?" I said, startled.

"They know better than that," Fleener said. "They don't tell us to stop. They tell us to ask questions, but don't offend the residents. Do the job, but don't upset people." I must have rolled my eyes. "I know, I know. Think I'd be here if I had another choice?"

"Don Hendricks is okay with this?" I asked again.

Fleener nodded. "Ask him if you don't believe me."

"I will," I said.

"Besides, you were the best idea we came up with."

"That's a ringing endorsement," I said. "Marty, I don't get it. Why don't you drag a couple of pompous asses from Cherokee Point into the office and sit them down for some old-fashioned interrogating?"

"Don't get me wrong, Michael," Fleener said, "we're doing our job, it's just . . . well, we're taking it slow. Trying to be diplomatic, you might say."

"Diplomatic? On a murder investigation? Does money and power buy that much?"

"Does Senator Randall Harrison of Indiana ring a bell? Or Congressman Gerald Van Der Mede?"

"You forgot former Governor Putnam," I said sarcastically.

Fleener ignored me. "Figure out who to talk to first. Cut down our list." I didn't say anything.

"Come on, Michael. Do I have to say 'please'?"

"Okay, okay," I said. "I'll see what I can do. Couple of friends I can start with. One's a retired lawyer from Chicago who's been on the Point all his life. The other is a good friend from law school, works for the Birmingham firm that handles legal business for the Point."

"Be a start," Fleener said.

"Am I acting as an agent of the police?"

"Not officially, no," Fleener said, shaking his head.

"So I'm just a guy asking questions?"

Fleener nodded and sipped some coffee.

"Got a few questions for you first," I said.

Fleener nodded again.

"Lotta rumors going around," I said. "Guy named Sheridan found the body. That right?"

"Yeah," Fleener said. "Kelsey Sheridan. At the tennis court."

"Signs of a struggle?"

"Nope. Abbott was face down. Slacks and sports coat were clean except for blood at the base of his skull. At the shirt collar."

"Think he knew the shooter?" I said.

"Probably. Cherokee Point's not easy to get into except the main gate."

"Find the gun?"

Fleener shook his head. "Not yet. One bullet did the job. Entered the base of the skull. Moderate angle up. No powder burns. But we're sure the shooter and the victim were only a few feet apart."

"Why?"

"Ballistics said the gun's a .25 caliber Browning, called a 'baby' Browning. Not very accurate. Unless you're close." Fleener rubbed his eyes. "We'll find the gun sooner or later. Could have been a few more bullets scattered in the woods, but I doubt it. Nobody heard anything."

"Anybody see him that night?"

"Lots of people," Fleener said. "Big cocktail party at the Harrison cottage. He was there. People saw him. No one knew why he went to the tennis court so late."

"Not much help," I said.

"Nope, but you never know." Fleener put his mug on the desk. "Thanks for the coffee," he said. "I'll email you a summary this afternoon." He got out of his chair and we shook hands. "Thanks, Michael."

Well, that was more interesting than my usual morning. Mostly I do domestic legal work. Divorces, probate, some tax issues. That sort of thing. I often ask my own questions, do my own investigating. In a small town, you learn to multi-task. That's never included investigating a murder.

2

I met Bill Stapleton in 1993, our first year in law school, in Ann Arbor. We'd grown up in suburban Detroit. Billy in Birmingham, me in Royal Oak. Two twenty-three year olds overwhelmed by "one L," as the first year in law school was called. Survival made us good friends. He was headed for Pennington, Gray and Stapleton, the Birmingham firm run by his father. I came along because it was the only offer I had. I always wanted to live in Petoskey. I dreamed of skiing Boyne Country in the winter and spending summers around the lakes like Nick Adams did in Hemingway's short stories, but I couldn't earn a living "Up North" fresh out of law school.

By 1998, after two years of billing hours in Birmingham, I inherited just enough money from a dead uncle to put a down payment on the Lake Street building. Thanks to Billy and his father, the firm agreed that I could take three clients with me who liked the idea of local legal consultations. I set up my office on the second floor and rented the street level space to a shoe business from Mackinac Island, the Mackinac Sandal Company. Retainers from the clients and rent from the store were enough to get "Michael Russo, Attorney at Law, L.L.C." off the ground.

But back to Billy.

"Line two," Sandy said.

"Good morning, Billy," I said, "how's things on the Woodward strip?"

"Same as the last time you asked me," he said. "Must be almost spring up there? Now that it's June."

"Very funny." I stood up and leaned against the window casing. The sun shimmered off the water in Little Traverse Bay two blocks away. "You're still jealous that I moved north and you didn't."

"Yeah, yeah," Stapleton said, "I hear you. But if I lived 'Up North,' could I spend an hour or two this afternoon looking at new Porsches?"

"Guy lives around the corner from me's got a beautiful black Targa. A '73. Never restored. He'd let you ogle it. If you don't touch."

"Now who's being funny," he said. "You know, Michael, I think about it a lot. I really do. Sally and I spend enough time up there, that's for sure. Mackinac Island in the summer. Petoskey and Harbor, too, especially in the winter." He hesitated for a minute. "But I don't imagine you called to offer me a partnership in your one-man operation."

"No, I didn't," I said, "but I bet we'd have fun. Listen, Billy, Pennington, Gray still works for Cherokee Point Resort, doesn't it?"

"Sure does."

"You read about the murder out there last week?"

"Sure did," Stapleton said. "Television, what's left of our newspapers. Hard to miss."

"Let me tell you why I called." I filled him in on my conversation with Captain Fleener. "I'm not asking for privileged information, but who should I talk to first? Better yet, is there someone who'll talk to me at all?"

"You probably know the people better than I do. I meet with the Board of Directors four times a year, but Wardcliff Griswold is the only one I talk to regularly."

"Wardcliff?" I said.

"Yep. First name is the surname of a previous generation. Lot of that going around at ole Cherokee Point. Ward is the president of the Association and the Board."

"Think he'd talk to me? If you asked him to?"

"He would if I asked, but the guy's wound pretty tight, Michael. Don't expect too much."

"Meaning what?"

"We took the resort as a client five years ago. I'm up there regularly for meetings with the Board. Ward pulled me aside once and said that it would be inappropriate for me, the attorney for the Point, to stay at the Griswold house when I'm in town."

"You wouldn't ask to stay with him," I said. "I don't get it."

"I never asked Griswold if I could stay at his house, Michael. He must assume everyone wants a piece of his life."

"If you say so. He sounds like a pretty strange guy."

"Uh-huh. I'll call Ward this afternoon. Tell him to expect your call."

"Thanks," I said. "Let me know if you get a new Porsche."

He gave me Griswold's unlisted phone number and I asked Sandy to call him in the morning to arrange a time. "Wardcliff?" she asked.

"Yep."

Meanwhile, I found Frank Marshall's number in my contacts list and punched the keypad. Marshall retired as the in-house investigator for a prominent Michigan Avenue law firm in Chicago in 2003. He'd been a visitor at Cherokee Point most of his life. When he and his wife decided to buy a home on the resort in 1999, he wanted a local attorney to handle the paperwork and hired me. We've been friends ever since.

"Michael, good to hear from you."

"Thanks, Frank," I said. "How's Ellen?"

"My lovely wife is just fine, thank you for asking. She's out on the bike trails right now, as a matter of fact."

"You running the Lilac Festival 10K on the Island on Saturday?" I said.

"You bet," Marshall said, "why don't you run it with me?"

"Hamstring's healing nicely," I said. "Only doing four miles right now. Don't want to push my luck. Let me know how you do."

"Be happy to."

"Say, Frank, you have time for breakfast in the morning? Like to tap your brain about the Point."

"Popular topic these days. What's your interest in Cherokee Point?"

"Might want to talk to some of your neighbors," I said.

"You helping the cops, Michael?"

"I'm a lawyer playing investigator, Frank. Sound familiar?"

"Any chance you're talking about the Abbott murder?"

"Uh-huh."

"Not a good idea, Michael."

walked into the Twisted Olive Café at nine the next morning. It's a small, pleasant place to eat and talk business. By the middle of next month, the tourists would be lined up waiting, not always patiently, for a table. But vacationers, who likely never heard of Nick Adams, had not arrived yet.

I said hello to Angela at the counter and pointed towards Frank Marshall at a table by a window.

"Good morning, Michael," Marshall said. We shook hands and I sat down. "Good choice to come here. Good food and the view ain't bad either." The restaurant sat on the bluff overlooking Little Traverse Bay and the breakwater. The beauty of the water was more obvious here than from my office. The big, white lakefront cottages of Harbor Springs across the bay stood in sharp contrast to a backdrop of dark green pine trees.

"Coffee and water, Mr. Russo?" our waitress asked.

"Yes, please."

"You're looking well, Michael. Haven't seen A.J. in a while. How is the love of your life?"

"Haven't seen her much lately, either," I said. "She's been pushing pretty hard at work. Big changes are coming and she wants to get it right." Audrey Jean Lester, called A.J. since high school in Lansing, worked at the *Petoskey Post Dispatch*. She's editor of the online version of the paper, *PPD Wired*, a constantly evolving project.

"Been training for the Lilac 10K, Frank?" I asked.

"Just want to run it," Marshall said. "I've tried to extend my longest run for the last few weeks, but that's about it. I hope to finish in the top three in my age group."

The waitress stopped at our table. "Ready to order or would you like more time?"

"I'm ready," Marshall said. "I'll have the omelet of the day and a small orange juice." I ordered Eggs Monaco, a variation on Eggs Benedict.

"Michael, I'll talk running all day, but you mentioned Cherokee Point. Playing investigator, are you?"

I nodded. "I visit the Point from time to time. Got a few clients, but you and Ellen are my only real friends out there. You've been residents all your life. I want to know what the place is like. Your impressions—good, bad or indifferent."

"Mind if I ask what the cops had to say?"

"Of course not," I said. I told Marshall about my conversation with Captain Fleener.

"Sounds more like playing cop than playing investigator," he said. "You think it's a good idea? You're an officer of the court, after all."

"Despite how it sounds, I'm not playing cop. This is more personal favor than official action."

"A favor to whom?" Marshall said. "Marty Fleener?"

"And Don Hendricks," I said. "I've had my share of run-ins with Hendricks, but I respect the guy. Marty's a good friend. They wouldn't ask if they didn't have to."

"Not sure it's as clean as you think. But let's put that aside for now. What can I do?"

"You know Bill Stapleton? From Pennington, Gray?" I said.

Marshall nodded.

"Billy gave me Wardcliff Griswold's name. Said he'd call Griswold on my behalf, but I thought I'd start with you. Might help me ask better questions."

"Ah, Wardcliff," he said. A small grin appeared on Marshall's face and he nodded slowly. "Actually, Ward's a pretty decent guy. A strange priority list, that's all. Privacy is paramount to him. People on the resort come first. He's the perfect guy to carry on for the founding generation. They call themselves 'the original four.'"

"That's a nice segue for some Cherokee Point history," I said.

The waitress brought two white plates with our breakfasts to the table. And more coffee.

"I'll give you a condensed version," Marshall said. "Ask questions, if you want."

"I'm all ears," I said, forking some eggs.

Marshall leaned back in his chair. He cut into his omelet and took a bite. "The feta cheese and the spinach," he said, using his knife to point at the omelet, "they get it right." Marshall looked at me. "Ever had this?"

I shook my head. "Cherokee Point?"

He sipped some coffee. "Almost a hundred years ago, 1919, four friends, all successful businessmen, bought an enormous chunk of waterfront and founded Cherokee Point Resort Association. Named it after the navigational map point. Harley Abbott, Thomas Griswold . . ."

"As in Wardcliff?" I said.

Marshall nodded. "Abbott, Griswold, Gerald Buchanan from Chicago and Roger Sheridan from Indianapolis. The original four families. They divided the land into forty lakefront lots and offered them to friends. Built huge homes. Called 'em cottages." Marshall smiled and cut another bite of omelet. "The emphasis was always on tranquility, civility and privacy. An elegant time back then, Michael. A very cautious world."

He flagged our waitress and pointed at his empty coffee cup.

"They created a Board of Directors to run the place through a manager. Never been more than a rubber stamp for the original four. Those guys control all the property and they have all the votes. The board can do what it likes, but the families run the show, especially the Abbotts."

"Abbott has more control than the others?"

"Uh-huh," Marshall said, "especially since the Buchanans left the Point. Ellen and I bought the Buchanan cottage, remember?"

I nodded. "But why Abbott and not one of the others?"

"Money," Marshall said emphatically. "The families wanted sequestered, controlled lives. The obsessive need for privacy. But they respect money and the Abbotts are serious money."

"Really?"

"Really," Marshall said. "The Abbott family put its money into timberland after the Civil War. Washington state, Louisiana and Northern Michigan. The U.P., too." Marshall ate some toast and followed it with coffee. "Abbott lumber built cities all over the country. Not just in the war-ravaged South, but Chicago, Pittsburgh, Philadelphia. Housing for migrants moving north for work. European immigrants, too. Made tons of money. Over the years, the Abbotts became the first among equals. Carleton carried on in good family tradition."

Our waitress poured more coffee. "Anything else, gentlemen?" We said no.

"Do the kids take over now that Carleton's dead?" I said.

"Nick'll take over, not Parker. Real brats, those two. Easy to forget they're in their forties."

"Why the son and not the daughter?" I said.

"Ah, now we get closer to it." I must have looked confused. "Think for a minute, Michael. No one wants the cops to ask questions, so the cops come to you. No one wants a local law firm, so a Birmingham firm represents the Point. Same thing applies to the Point's accountants in Grand Rapids. The son will inherit the Abbott fortune, not the daughter. It's about tradition. It's about privacy. It's about 1919. A healthy dose of paranoia, too."

"I don't get it."

"No, I guess you don't." Marshall said. "Look, Michael, Cherokee Point is a very conservative place."

"Meaning politically?" I said.

"Sure, but political in the larger perspective-on-the-world sense." Marshall pushed his plate to the side and folded his napkin. "For the last twenty-five years, a small group of us have been derisively referred to as the 'goddamn fucking liberals' for supporting Democratic candidates. But if you focus on elections, you miss the importance of conservative tradition, of how the world should function."

Marshall looked out the window. Heavy clouds were moving in from the west. Rain would follow.

"Michael, try this. Bill Clinton's liberal politics in the '92 campaign were vilified. No surprise there. But the key to understanding the world of Cherokee Point was the reaction to Hillary Rodham Clinton. Smart, tenacious, outspoken. Remember the dust-up over Hillary's comments about standing by her man and baking cookies?"

"The Tammy Wynette thing."

"Exactly. Well, that really set people off. Policies are easy to argue or dismiss, but the way you live your life? Not as easy if it offends you, if you feel threatened. Oh and she works for a living."

"They don't like that Hillary has a career?" I said.

"In a word, no," Marshall said. "The only women at the Point who worked real jobs or had careers were . . ."

"The goddamn fucking liberals."

"Now you're beginning to understand."

"Okay, but what's that got to do with Fleener and Hendricks?"

"At Cherokee Point, paranoia lives just below the surface. Anything and everything threaten their world. A presidential candidate's spouse, the locals in town, now a murder investigation. They believe other people, especially local folks, want to know their business. Locals, like cops, like medical people. They're crawling all over the place because of the murder. They must stop people from prying into their lives. Their world is crumbling and they're desperately trying to hold it together. A murder investigation is just an excuse for people to find out about their lives."

"Boy, that is paranoid," I said.

Marshall nodded and sipped the last of his orange juice. "The truth is that their lives are rather unremarkable. Local folks could care less, they have their own lives to worry about, but try to convince the members of Cherokee Point Resort Association of that."

"Man, you live with a strange bunch." I said.

He smiled, but it was not a humorous smile.

"Would they cover up a murder?"

"We talked to the cops, Michael. All of us at the party."

"At the Harrison cottage?" I said.

Marshall nodded. "Last place Abbott was seen alive, as far as we know."

"Nobody had much to say about Abbott that night?" I asked.

"It was a cocktail party. What do you expect? Lotta booze."

"Abbott a drinker?"

Marshall nodded. "Big time," he said. "Fancied himself a ladies' man, too."

"So your neighbors will co-operate, but no more than they have to."

"Right. Their desire to keep the outside world away could overpower the desire to do their civic duty."

"I'll keep that in mind," I said.

"If you're going to ask questions on behalf of the cops, go slowly. Start with non-threatening questions. Maybe you can get my neighbors to relax. Might make it easier for Fleener to do his job."

"Maybe," I said.

"Don't overlook Kelsey Sheridan."

"The man who found the body?"

"Uh-huh," Marshall said. "Bright guy. Thoughtful, too. Talk to him. Doesn't think like the rest of them. Might be helpful."

"You gonna be my mentor?" I said.

"Consigliere," Marshall said, "like in *The Godfather*. I'll be your consigliere."

"Be sure to get me an enforcer like Luca Brasi," I said, "just in case."

"Don't be a smart-ass, Michael."

I picked up the check. "Breakfast's on me."

"No argument here."

We left the Café and walked across Bay Street to the parking lot.

"Thanks for the suggestions, Frank."

"Always enjoy our time together, whatever the reason." We stopped at Marshall's black Audi S-4. He beeped the door locks.

"Nice ride, my friend, nice ride."

"When you talk to Wardcliff Griswold, go slow. Get back to me afterward."

4

I crossed the parking lot and went in the rear entrance of the McLean & Eakin bookstore.

"Good morning, Mr. Russo," said the woman at the desk. "Got your *New York Times* right here."

"Thanks," I said and paid for the paper. I left by the front door and walked four doors down Lake Street to my office.

"Good morning, Fran," I said to the woman sweeping the sidewalk in front of my building. "How's the sandal business today?"

"Let you know later," she said. Fran Warren is a smart, attractive woman in her early fifties. A trim five-seven with soft blond hair usually pulled into a ponytail, she stays in shape riding a bike or walking on the hilly streets of Petoskey. Warren opened her first store on Mackinac Island in 1995, then leased from me three years later when she decided that it was more appealing to live in Petoskey in the winter. She kept a small apartment on the Island for the summer tourist season. "If the weather's good this summer, business will follow," she said. "Here and on the Island."

"You going up for the Lilac Festival?"

"Working a water stop for the 10K Saturday. I'll stay a few days."

"Have fun," I said. The door to my office was next to the Sandal Company's door. I climbed the stairs to the second floor.

"Good morning, Michael," Sandy said. "Your mail's on the desk. And I printed off a copy of the police report on the Abbott murder."

"You read it?" I asked.

"Yep."

"What do you think?"

"About the murder or Cherokee Point?"

"Both," I said and pointed to my office.

"We'll need coffee," she said.

Sandy came in, handed me a mug of coffee and sat down. I leaned back in my chair and drank some. "I ever said you make good coffee?"

"All the time, but thanks again."

"Back to the report," I said.

"I've read enough police reports," she said. "I get the idea even if I don't understand all the jargon." She picked up the report and turned to an inside page. "Here's the gist of it. A sheriff's car responds to a call from Cherokee Point. A resident, named Kelsey Sheridan, found the body at the tennis court. Turned out to be Carleton Abbott with a bullet hole in the back of his head. Another patrol car shows up. Responding to the original call most likely. One of the officers must have called in, because before you know it, State Police detectives show up."

"Pretty quick for the staties," I said.

"That's what I thought," Sandy said. "Then, just like that, Captain Martin Fleener's knocking on your door."

"Seem like veteran cops wanted to hand the dead guy to somebody else?"

"Looks that way," she said. "They're so desperate, they came to you."

"Thanks a lot," I said. "Pumps my confidence level."

"You're welcome. More coffee?"

"Yeah," I said. Sandy handed me the report and went for the coffee. I made a note to call the prosecutor's office. Don Hendricks seemed to sit somewhere between the Sheriff, the State Police and Cherokee Point.

"Tell me about Cherokee Point," I said to Sandy after we had more coffee. "Frank Marshall just gave me a history lesson over breakfast. Made some odd comments, too. You've lived around here all your life. What do you think?"

Sandy shifted uncomfortably in her chair. "The place, well, it's always been there. Driven by it, but never been inside. I know who some of the people are, of course. Like the Abbotts. I don't have any friends out there."

Sandra Jefferies grew up in Emmet County. She was married once, a long time ago. In 2008, after her mother died, she moved into her father's two-story near Crooked Lake, just north of town, to take care of him.

"No friends?"

She shook her head.

"I don't get that," I said.

She shifted uncomfortably again.

"Sandy," I said, "you're fidgeting."

"It's not easy to talk about, I guess," she said. "Most of the people out there are from down-state. They don't have a lot in common with the commoners."

"I'm from down-state, Sandy," I said. "I'm a runner and you think that's nuts. You read every sci-fi novel to hit the shelves, I can't waste my time on sci-fi. You eat veggie everything, I need a good cheeseburger now and then. You frown on some of the people we take as clients. We don't have a lot in common."

"That's not what I mean."

"Then what do you mean? Are they snobs? Is that it?"

"I suppose so," she said, "but that's not the point. You remember I worked a lot of years at the bank?" She pointed in the general direction of up the street.

"Uh-huh."

"I baby-sat accounts, took care of problems. That sort of thing. Lots of Cherokee Point people over the years. Look, this is a resort town and snobs are a dime a dozen in the summer. But the people out there aren't very nice. I'm not the only one who thinks so. They don't care about the people who live here, work here. No respect for any of us." Sandy picked up her coffee mug, but put it down without taking a swallow. "They move up here and do as they please. Like they own the town."

"I moved up here and do as I please, too," I said.

"Goddammit, Michael, you're a decent guy. You treat everyone with respect." I started to say something, but Sandy put out her hand, like a traffic cop and stopped me. "Fran downstairs. The guy with the piercings who makes sandwiches at Roast & Toast. Some of the nut-jobs who come in here trying to hire you. They're all people to you."

"But how did you know that I . . ."

"I knew right away when you interviewed me for this job," she said.

"But how . . ."

"For one thing," she said, "you didn't treat me like a stupid broad."

"Oh."

"More important, you listened to what I had to say. Still do. Most of the time, anyway," she said, with a crooked smile.

"Think that'll help me win over the folks at Cherokee Point?"

"Gonna find out soon enough," she said. "Wardcliff Griswold expects you at his house tomorrow at eleven."

5

I put my feet up on the corner of the desk. The dark sky hung low over the bay. A few raindrops softly hit the window. More would come soon. Other clients needed attention, but first I picked up my cell phone and shot a quick text to A.J. "Dinner tonight?"

I took two files from the right-hand top drawer. Jane Friedman was about to close on an old farmhouse south of town, on the Charlevoix Road. Easy enough. The paperwork was done except for the inspection report. Robin Savage was divorcing her husband. Neither party was interested in a gunfight. Depositions were not yet scheduled, so that was on hold. The rest of my clients thought I was terrific because they seldom needed to call me.

"Michael," I heard Sandy say from the front room, "Don Hendricks is on line one."

I picked up the phone. "Hello, Don. What's up?"

"I want you in my office today. After lunch."

"Good morning to you, too," I said sarcastically. I heard my cell phone chime.

"Sorry, counselor," he said. "Bad ass day. How 'bout it? Two o'clock?"

"I'll be there," I said and hung up, then picked up my cell and swiped the screen. It lit up with A.J.'s response, "Chandler's at 6:30." That brought a smile to my face. Long hours at the paper meant less time for us and I missed her.

I got up and went into the front office. "You eating in or out today?" I asked.

"Brought a sandwich and potato salad. Trying to finish *The Big Sleep*," she said. "You read it?"

"Uh-huh," I said, "You figure out the plot?"

"Of course not," she said. "Still a fun read, though."

I grabbed my *Times*, went downstairs and dodged the raindrops to get the half block to the Roast & Toast. Inside, the restaurant looked like an urban coffee house with its high ceiling, industrial tin and colorful neon. I got a bowl of pea soup and an iced tea and sat at a small two-top in the front window.

I opened the newspaper, but I spent more time staring out at Lake Street. Getting caught up in a murder investigation was risky enough, but the people at Cherokee Point sounded like the Adams Family gone bad. Two people I trust offered a string of unflattering comments about Point members, to say the least. Add Marty Fleener to that and you've got a hat trick of arrogant, selfish behavior. Up next was Don Hendricks. Hard to tell what he'd have to say.

I finished my soup and went back to the office. I slipped the hard copy of the police report into my brief bag and put on my yellow rain slicker for the three-block walk to the County building. The rain was coming harder now, so I zipped the slicker up tight around my neck and pulled the hood around my face. Another early summer day in Petoskey. But as the cliché says, "Don't like the weather? Wait five minutes."

Hendricks was waiting for me when I got to his office.

"Come on in," he said and closed the door behind us. His office was quietly institutional. Muted color, muted carpet, muted furniture. Hendricks' chair sat by the window so he could swivel around and look out on the street. I sat in a straight-backed chair across from the desk.

"You want anything?" Hendricks asked. "Coffee or water?"

"Nothing," I said. "Thanks."

"Okay, then, let's get to it." Don Hendricks was a no-nonsense guy. He didn't take bullshit easily, didn't often give it either. He was serving his second term as county prosecuting attorney. In his late fifties, Hendricks was an imposing man. He stood six-two and weighed about two-thirty, but it was soft pounds and it showed in his puffy face and close-cut brown hair. He didn't wear suits well. He looked rumpled even in the morning.

"How you feel about helping us out on the Abbott murder?" he asked.

"About as hot for the idea as you, I imagine." I hesitated for a minute, but Hendricks stayed quiet. "You and Fleener must be under a lot of pressure to cook up a plan like this."

"Look, Russo," he said, "you don't have to do this."

"I told Marty I'd see what I could find out. I'm telling you the same thing. I'm in it. For now, anyway."

"What's that mean?" he said, "'for now'?"

"Take it easy," I said. "I only mean this is a murder case and it's your case. We've had our differences over the years, Don, but I don't want to do anything stupid to mess this up." Hendricks' shoulders sagged a bit, as if it were hard to accept my help. Or hard to acknowledge that he needed outside help.

"I gotta put limits on you," he said.

"Tell me."

"Don't try to be a cop when you're out there."

"Never occurred to me," I said.

"Ask questions. Gotta be some people more worth talkin' to than others. Who are they? Who really knew Abbott and the rest of the family? Get us a few good names. Most important, put them at ease so Fleener can get somewhere."

"That's a pretty strange bunch. Not sure how much I can get them to open up for you guys."

"I don't care if they're lunatics from fuckin' Mars. I've got a job to do. But every time I try to do it, I get a call from some asshole with too much time on his hands and too much power." Hendricks' face was red. He was not a happy man. "You know Senator Harrison? Randall Harrison from Indiana?"

"Met him. Don't know him. He on your case?"

"On my ass be a better way to put it. And Congressman Gerald Van Der Mede." Hendricks dragged out each part of the man's name. "From downstate. Near Grand Rapids. No direct threats. Nothing so obvious. Nothing that might be taken as obstructing a murder investigation." Hendricks shook his head slowly. He looked out the window, then back at me. "But it's the way they say things. Be nice to the poor folks at Cherokee Point. Don't get too rough on them."

"Harrison and Van Der Mede made their own calls?"

"You bet. Wanted me to know who has the clout."

"Got a couple of questions for you," I said.

Hendricks nodded.

"You read the police report?"

He nodded again.

"What's not in the report?"

"You're a smart guy, Russo," Hendricks said, "but it's all there."

"I might want to talk to the first County cops on the scene. Or the coroner."

"Lemme know. I'll arrange it." Hendricks reached for a manila file on his desk. "Here's one thing not in the report. Came later." He handed me a single sheet of paper, a copy of a letter to him. Eleven men signed the letter. "Recognize any of those guys?"

"Several are familiar. Know two of them. They all Cherokee Point?" Hendricks nodded. I started to read the letter.

"I'll save you the trouble," he said. "The gist of the thing is that each of these charming fellows has retained a lawyer. I want to talk to 'em, it says, call their lawyer. I want to ask questions? Ask the lawyer. I want to piss on all of them, that's what I want to do. Piss on the lawyers first."

"Is that so?"

"Shut up, Russo," he said without the slightest inflection. "These names," he took the paper back, "could be a place to start."

"You got a suspect?" I asked.

"Family," Hendricks said. "One of the kids, Nickelson or Parker. Nick'd be my guess. Don't know which one inherits daddy's bucks."

"It's Nick," I said. Hendricks stared at me for a second.

"You know this how?"

"Good sources," I said. "Tradition says that only the men win at Cherokee Point." Hendricks came out of his chair slowly, deliberately and walked around the desk. My time must be up. He stopped near my chair, leaned back on the front edge of the desk and folded his beefy arms across his chest.

"One more thing," he said. "Got a call the other day from a guy I know in Lansing. Organized crime task force. He'd heard about Abbott."

"Cherokee Point's a retirement home for the mob?"

"Shut up." Hendricks said, again, with no irony at all. "Joey DeMio ring a bell?"

"Don't think so."

"Carmine DeMio, maybe?"

"Him I recognize," I said. "Chicago mob, right?"

Hendricks nodded. "Carmine's retired or so they say and son Joey's taken over the old man's money and drug operation."

"The kid just takes over? Nobody objects?"

"Daddy's muscle works for Joey now."

I nodded my head slowly. "And why am I being treated to this reprise of *The Godfather*?"

"Jesus, Russo, haven't you seen any other movies?"

"*The Godfather, Part II.*"

"Shut up," Hendricks said. "Look, Nickelson Abbott likes to lose money. Blackjack, the ponies, college basketball. Owes a lot of money. Guess who?"

"Joey DeMio."

"Bingo," Hendricks said. "Gets his drugs from DeMio, too. Weed mostly. Some pills. Plus, Joey's got something going with Parker Abbott."

"Gambling? Drugs?"

"Not sure. Hot to get in her pants, for sure. Joey spends a lot of time at Cherokee Point."

"How do you run wiseguys in the Windy City from Northern Michigan?"

"Good question," Hendricks said.

"He stay with Parker?"

Hendricks nodded. "Or at his father's hotel on Mackinac Island. Carmine's got a big house there, too. On the East Bluff."

I looked at Hendricks. "If Nick inherits the money, he pays a lot of bills."

Hendricks nodded. "Good motive for murder."

6

Sandy left the office shortly after five. I finished editing notes from an interview with a perspective client who wanted to hire me to sue his former business partner who'd looted the company bank accounts and took off for Canada. Calgary, he thought. I told him he ought to call the Mounties, but I'd see what I could do.

The afternoon rain had called it quits. Small patches of blue were tucked into the dark gray sky hanging over the bay. Could make for a sunny run in the morning. Get me in shape to meet the esteemed President of Cherokee Point.

I put the client notes into my brief bag, grabbed my rain slicker and headed down the stairs to meet A.J.

I'll always be pulled by the energy of big cities, but in Petoskey I can walk. My apartment is a block down Howard Street from Chandler's, which is another block around the corner from my office. A.J.'s house is three blocks up Bay Street from both places. Petoskey's a small town if you only count people, but those people are warm and friendly. More important, they like living here and it shows.

Chandler's is a charming restaurant tucked into a courtyard. Shaped like a rectangle, the bar is on the left. Tables line the other wall. I spotted A.J. at a small table near the back. She waved.

"Hey, Michael, how ya doing tonight?" It was Jack behind the bar. In his fifties, Jack looked more like a jockey than a bartender. Small, wiry, tightly packed. You'd check his ID if not for the close cut salt and pepper hair.

"Evening, Jack." Two attractive women, both brunettes, one with celebrity cleavage, sat with a smartly dressed man at the bar. The man was Tom Preston, a real estate broker from town. The women were fresh faces. Tom paid no attention to me. Go Tom.

A.J. wore a very business-like navy blazer over a white blouse with gray linen slacks. I leaned over and gave her a soft kiss on the lips.

"Hmm, that feels nice," she said. "We haven't had a lot of time these past few months."

I put my slicker over the chair, dropped my bag on the floor and sat down.

"You gotta big project," I said. Audrey Jean Lester graduated from Journalism School at Michigan State in 1993. Her first job was part-time on the rewrite desk and part-time as a reporter for the *Lansing State Journal*. She came to Petoskey in 2000 as a reporter for the *Post Dispatch*, two years after I opened my practice.

We met that first summer because she was writing a story about professionals who moved north to live and work. I couldn't take my eyes off her while she asked me questions over coffee at Julienne Tomatoes. Tall at about five-nine, A.J. had an angular face and jet-black hair she pushed behind her ears. It curled softly at her shirt collar. On that morning she'd worn tan slacks, a soft rose blouse and a loosely tied scarf at her neck. I tried hard to examine her body without being obvious. When she got more coffee, I concluded that she filled out the slacks very nicely. After our first meeting, I kept calling with more information for her story. One afternoon she walked into my office and said, "Why don't you cut the bullshit and we go on a date?"

"Fixing the online edition was a much bigger project than I thought," she said. "When I saw the early versions of it, I knew the guys didn't get it. They jumped on the electronic bandwagon without thinking it through first." A.J. slowly shook her head.

"How do you feel now?" I asked.

"We're getting there," she said. "We're getting there."

Our waiter came to the table. "A.J., Michael, good evening. Can I get you wine or spirits tonight?" We nodded simultaneously.

"Chardonnay, please, Andrew," A.J. said.

"Dewer's on the rocks for me."

"Will do. We've got sea bass tonight, by the way. Comes with a balsamic reduction, duchess potatoes and a vegetable. It's even better than the last time you had it, Michael."

"Thanks, Andrew," I said.

When our waiter left, A.J. asked, "How'd your talk with Hendricks go?"

I filled her in. "He was clear what he wants from me." I handed A.J. a copy of the names Hendricks had given me. "I cut that list, the cops have a better place to start."

"I recognize some of these names," she said.

"From Cherokee Point or someplace else?"

"Both," she said. "I used to cover civic functions. A lot of these guys would be there."

"Anyway, soften up a few of the residents for real cop questions."

"Are you staring at my chest?" she said quietly.

"I am, indeed," I said. "Been missing your body lately."

"Glad to hear it," she said. "Now back to Hendricks."

Andrew put our drinks on the table with a basket of bread. "Ready to order?"

"You sold me," A.J. said, "the sea bass."

"Me, too." Andrew left and I raised my glass, "Here's lookin' at you, my dear."

"Hendricks?" she said and clinked my glass.

"Heard of Carmine DeMio? Joey DeMio?"

She looked at me with her mouth open. "Of course I've heard of them," she said.

"Because you're a reporter?"

"Because I live here," she said. "You don't have to be a reporter to know when a Chicago wiseguy buys a cottage on Mackinac Island. Great gossip for weeks."

Andrew put two plates of well-presented food on the table. A.J. ordered another Chardonnay. I joined her.

"Would you recognize Carmine or Joey?"

"Sure," she said, then took a bite of sea bass. "Good fish."

"Hendricks said something's going on between Joey and Parker Abbott."

A.J. shook her head slowly. "Michael, you really need to get out more. I'm surprised the infamous couple isn't here now." I looked over at the bar. Tom Preston was still there. One woman was gone. Tom and the brunette with cleavage were getting to know each other a lot better. "Is there anything else you'd like to know?" A.J. said sarcastically.

I nodded. "Does a retired mob guy look at houses for sale in the window at Mackinac Island Realty, pick one out and drop a suitcase full of cash on the desk?"

"That'd be the movies," A.J. said. "This was a private purchase."

I caught Andrew's eye and ordered another round of drinks.

"DeMio bought the Brewster cottage. The Brewester family was four, five generations on the island. Oil in Texas or maybe Oklahoma." Andrew set fresh drinks at our table. "Anyway, he died and Catherine Brewster kept the place four more years. Then sold to DeMio."

"How did the widow know a Mafia big shot?"

"No one knows how they met. Or when. She sold her cottage to DeMio and bought a pied-a-terre in Paris to live and paint." A.J. sipped her wine. "Any more questions?"

"You like the bass?" She said nothing but discretely stuck her tongue out. "Know anything about Joey DeMio and Nick Abbott?"

"Other than Joey feeds Nickelson's gambling habit?"

"I give up," I said, tossing my hands in the air.

"Maybe you should. Stick to wills and divorces," she said. "You sure Hendricks isn't holding out on you?"

I faked astonishment. "A prosecutor holding out?"

A.J. rolled her eyes.

"I'm not sure of anything," I said.

"Will there be anything else?" Andrew asked as he cleared our plates.

"No, thanks," I said. I put a credit card on the table.

"You decide to talk to Joey DeMio or Carmine, don't approach either one on the street."

"Okay," I said. "Why not?"

"A very large bodyguard is never far away."

"Got more tidbits I oughta know?"

"My chest looks even better without clothes on."

"Yes, it does," I said. "Your place or mine?"

"Your apartment is closer."

7

"What time is it?"

"I dunno," I said.

"You're staring at the clock."

"Doesn't mean I'm looking at it." I tried to roll over, but A.J.'s legs were tangled in mine. "You kept me up too long last night," I said. "Ouch! Don't pinch!"

"No bad puns before coffee," she said. "Against the house rules."

"It's my house," I protested.

"Doesn't matter." A.J. threw back the sheet. "It's seven. Gotta go home and get ready for work. Another long day, I'm afraid." She swung her feet over the side of the bed and reached for her camisole on the floor.

"Want me to help?"

A.J. shook her head. "Your job is to take it off. A task you preformed quite expertly last night, I might add." She pulled the camisole over her head and adjusted it, then stood. She picked up her pants and blouse. "Wished I'd hung 'em up."

"Dinner tonight?" I said.

"Can't tell," she said. "I'll call or text. You're talking to Griswold later, right?"

I nodded. "Oughta be interesting."

"Running this morning?"

"A short four," I said. "Give me time to think about Griswold."

"I'm jealous. Haven't done a long walk in, what, a week. No bike either." A.J. kissed me, "See ya," she said, and walked out of the bedroom. I heard the door close.

I sat on the edge of the bed, grabbed my boxers and put them on. I opened the blinds. The sun was up and the sky was a clear blue. Nice morning. I went to the kitchen, got coffee out of the freezer, put six scoops into the Mr. Coffee and filled the tank with water.

While the coffee brewed, I went to the closet near the apartment door. Inside I kept a small two-drawer chest for running clothes. I opened the top drawer and took out a yellow poly T-shirt. I swapped my boxers for a pair of black running shorts.

I poured a mug of coffee and took it to the living room couch. I'd moved into the apartment when I'd come to town in 1999. The two-story building sat on Rose Street, behind the Perry-Davis Hotel, and the living room window had a modest view of the bay. Every time I think about a larger place, I sit in this room and say to myself, "I like it here."

I finished my coffee, laced up my Asics shoes and walked down the stairs. The air was already warm as I headed up Rose to Arlington. That'd take me into the quiet, tree-lined streets of Bay View, a Methodist summer community filled with gingerbread cottages. Most of the activity this early in the summer came from painters and construction people. It'd be easier to focus on Griswold with few cars around. Fifty minutes later, with a comfortable sweat worked up, I clicked my watch off and walked the last hundred yards to my building. Guess I ran over five. Got too wrapped up in Griswold.

My best shot was to convince him that I was there to help the residents deal with Fleener and Hendricks, not the other way around. Then he might be okay with the people talking to me. That, of course, would help Hendricks and Fleener. Get me back to wills and divorces sooner, too.

After a quick shower and more coffee, I put on khaki pants, a blue button-down shirt and navy blazer —what lawyers from resort-land should wear for summer business meetings. "President Griswold, sir, I am your humble servant, here to help your people at this difficult time."

An English muffin popped in the toaster. I slathered on raspberry jam and poured the last of the coffee into my mug. That's the plan. Help Wardcliff Griswold and the goofy folks at Cherokee Point keep the mean ole cops away.

I took a bottle of water from the refrigerator, picked up my brief bag and left for the parking lot by the back entrance. My dark blue 3-Series sat in the third spot down from the door. Porsche-lover Billy Stapleton sarcastically approved of my BMW because it was all-wheel drive and I lived in snow country. Nice of him. I beeped the locks, tossed my bag on the back seat and hung my jacket on the roof hook.

I pulled out of the lot and followed the same route I'd just run until I left Arlington for U.S. 31. as it ran along Little Traverse Bay. Traffic had picked up noticeably since Memorial Day weekend, especially near the restaurants and bars north of town. It would get thicker in a week or so when vacation season really got going. I turned onto the Harbor-Petoskey Road. It curved its way around to State Road, passing the airport and a health club, a couple of miles outside of downtown Harbor Springs.

I stopped for the light at State Road and turned north. Once you passed the two ski resorts and a large condo complex, the territory becomes rural Northern Michigan very fast. The hills crowded with skiers in the winter are now long stretches of grass divided into ski trails by large groups of pine trees. I passed The Fish restaurant, not yet open for the season, turned left on Robinson and headed toward Lake Michigan. I ran over my meeting with Griswold one more time.

I turned left on North Lake Shore, drove south, watching for three flagpoles at the road's edge. After a few minutes I spotted a large grassy section carved out of the pine trees. The entrance to Cherokee Point. The flags, for the United States, Michigan and the resort itself, waved gently against the June breeze. I downshifted a gear, turned off the road and stopped in front of a large iron gate. A six-foot high fieldstone wall stretched out into the trees from either side of the gate as far as I could see. It looked like a fortress. A man in his thirties, neatly dressed in khakis and a blue polo shirt came out of the small, gray, clapboard gatehouse and walked up to the car. He carried a spiral notebook. Couldn't see if he also carried a gun.

"Good morning, sir," he said. His shirt read "Staff" on the left chest.

"Good morning," I said. "Michael Russo. Wardcliff Griswold's expecting me." He never looked at the notebook. But he didn't pull a gun either.

"Yes, sir," he said. "Do you know where President Griswold lives?"

I resisted the temptation to make a smart-ass comment. It was hard. Probably had backup in the gatehouse. "I know the house," I said, "been on the resort before."

"The Point, sir," he said, "we call it the Point."

"Got it," I said. "Thanks." Just got spanked by a guy with "Staff" on his shirt. Mr. Staff turned around and nodded at the gatehouse. The wrought iron in front of me slid silently into the trees. There was backup in that little building, after all.

Cherokee Point always impressed me with its beauty. There is green everywhere. Green grass, carefully manicured, took up the space between the blue water of Lake Michigan and the green trees of pine, oak and elm.

I eased my way down the dirt road, passing tennis courts, a raised wooden squash court and a one-floor log building used for meetings, dinners and parties. Name signs stood at the end of each driveway. I recognized a few from the list Hendricks had given me. About three-quarters of a mile from the entrance, I turned in at the driveway marked, "Griswold." No dirt here. The drive and a small parking area were covered in tiny, very white stones. No weeds in the stones. I parked the BMW, gathered up my jacket and brief bag and followed the stone path to the back of the house. The front was the side that overlooked Lake Michigan.

Griswold's manor was a three-story Victorian with weathered gray siding and tall, skinny windows. A garage had been added to the rear of the house, but it matched the rest of the house in style and color.

A tall man, trim, in his sixties with short gray hair appeared around the corner. He wore a green cable-knit sweater over a crisp white shirt and tan corduroy pants with little green ducks on them. Where do they buy pants like that?

He waved. "Mr. Russo," he said, "welcome to the Point."

He put out his hand and I took it. "Thank you, Mr. Griswold," I said, figuring I'd better be formal, too. "Good to meet you. I appreciate your time."

"Think nothing of it," he said. "When Bill Stapleton asked me to speak with you, I hesitated at first. But what harm can it do? We're all friends, right?"

"Certainly," I said, never having laid eyes on the guy wearing duck pants before.

He gestured towards the front of the house. "Let's walk this way." And we did, around the side of the house to the front yard and its expansive view of the lake. "Beautiful, isn't it?"

I nodded.

"Nothing quite like it," he said. "Oh, the Riviera's more elegant, the Alps more thrilling. But this is home. Know what I mean?"

"It is beautiful, Mr. Griswold," I said.

"Let's dispense with the formality, shall we? It's Michael, is it not?"

"Yes,"

"And please call me Ward, if you would."

"All right, Ward," I said. Calling him Wardcliff probably wasn't a good idea. But I was tempted. I was feeling claustrophobic and I was outside, in a big front yard, next to a bigger lake.

Griswold pointed at the front door. "Shall we go inside?" We climbed three steps to the porch that stretched the width of the house. White wicker furniture, four high-back chairs and a couch, each with paisley seat cushions, took up space on the porch. Some magazines and several candles sat atop a wicker coffee table near the railing.

We went through the door and into the living room. It was big and square. Tall windows spanned the front of the room. A stairway up was off to the far side. A fieldstone fireplace rested on the back wall, rising up through the twelve-foot ceiling. More white wicker furniture was arranged around the fireplace. An antique hutch sat between a pair of large side windows and low bookshelves fitted under the window ledges around two sides of the room. A man stood next to the fireplace, posing like a Ralph Lauren ad. He was dressed more casually than either of us in faded jeans and a navy sweatshirt that said "Cherokee Point" across the front in big, white letters. Tan deck shoes. No socks. The man was six feet tall, stocky, with close cut brown hair. Probably in his late forties.

"Michael," Griswold said, "may I present Nickelson Abbott."

Without any obvious reaction, Abbott reached out to shake hands. "Call me Nick," he said.

"Pleased to meet you," I said.

"Let's all sit down," Griswold said, gesturing towards the chairs. "Shirlene?" he said to no one I could see. In the doorway leading to the back of the house, quietly appeared a short, thin black woman with plenty of gray laced into her hair. She wore khaki pants and a navy polo shirt. She also wore one of those white, frilly aprons that hung around the neck and tied around the waist. Couldn't tell if she, too, had "Staff" stitched on her shirt.

"Yes, sir?"

"Coffee for three," Griswold said, "and an assortment of the Danish you made this morning. Just in case the gentlemen are hungry."

"Yes, sir." She disappeared as quickly as she had appeared.

"Michael, I invited Nick to join us this morning. Clearly, he has a vested interest in solving our little problem."

I let that one go, "our little problem." Don't have to start a fight just yet. Might as well see where Griswold is going. "Will your sister be joining us?" I asked Nick.

"I speak for the family," he said.

"That so."

"It is," he said. "She's in mourning."

And you're not?

Shirlene came into the room carrying a large silver tray with blue on white china cups and saucers, a large carafe and a plate of mighty fine looking Danish. She put it on the coffee table.

"We'll serve ourselves, Shirlene," he said. And we did. I was the only one who picked up a Danish, strawberry and put it on a napkin. Before

I took a bite, Griswold said, "I hope we can agree on a reasonable way to solve our problem." There it was, again. I chewed my roll. Well done, Shirlene.

Abbott chimed in. "Ward wanted me here today, but I'm still not sure why." He drank some coffee. "There isn't anything to discuss, really. The old man's dead. The Point's got nothing to do with that."

"Well, now, Nick," Griswold said, "Carleton was found on the grounds."

"What I meant," Abbott said with an edge, "was that people here had nothing to do with his death. The cops have no reason to poke around the Point."

Our "little problem" was back. I noticed the portrait over the fireplace. Five or six feet high, three wide. A woman in her twenties, maybe, sitting in front of this fireplace, in one of these wicker chairs. She wore a long, blue, cotton floral dress. Very *Gone with the Wind*.

"Well, Nick, of course, I concur. Don't you, Michael?"

I came here planning to get Griswold to see my side of the "little problem." But they're trying the reverse on me.

"Michael? You agree, don't you," he asked again.

Gee, Wardcliff, no I don't. Well, here goes. "Gentlemen," I said, "This is a murder investigation. With due respect to your father," I said, nodding at Nick, "but Carleton Abbott was shot to death right here." Nick shrugged.

"Michael," Griswold said, "I'll tell you the same thing I told the State Police and that prosecutor, whatever his name. Tragic as this is, it has nothing to do with us."

"The police and Prosecutor Donald Hendricks don't see it that way, Ward. To them it's murder. They're just doing their job, after all."

"You sure about that?" Nick said.

"Yes, of course. From the County's point of view, it's just another case. A brutal one, but just another case."

"It's never 'another case' when the Point's involved," Nick said, sneering. "They oughta stop prying into our lives."

"I hoped that we might come to an agreement this morning," I said, trying to sound reasonable. "Let the cops talk to a few people, here, in this relaxed setting. Let them do their job and they'll be gone." I lied, of course. Not a chance in hell of that. Not when you got a guy with a bullet in the back of his head. But never mind. These guys were starting to annoy me. "You want the county out of the way? Answer their questions. Put an end to it."

Nick Abbott stood up. "Ward, I'm tired of this guy telling us what we should do." He dismissively waved his hand in my direction. This guy's got no feelings. None that I can see anyway.

"If we don't agree on some modified plan for the police," I said, "Captain Martin Fleener will be back here with more than a few officers and he will ask questions. Lots of questions. He'll talk to everybody. You know the drill. It won't stop until he stops. 'Where were you on the night of the murder? Who were you with? Got an alibi? How well did you know the dead man? Ever heard of Joey DeMio or Carmine DeMio?'" I tossed that last one in to see if it got a reaction.

"Not gonna happen, pal," Nick said. "I'm done with this guy, Ward. Good-bye." With that, a petulant Abbott walked out the front door and headed down the green lawn. No chance this guy would give the one-percent a good name. I glared at Griswold, but his face was without expression, as if he just looked up from his newspaper.

"Shirlene," Griswold said, "we're finished." Griswold stood up, turned to me, his growls sagging and said, "That will be all for now, Mr. Russo. Good day." He turned and went through the doorway to the back of the house just as Shirlene appeared. "Show the gentleman out, Shirlene." I heard him say.

"No need, ma'am," I said, "I can find my way." When I got to the front door, I looked back at Shirlene who was picking up cups and napkins. "Shirlene." Her eyes barely moved in my direction.

"Sir?"

"Good Danish."

8

What the hell had I gotten myself into? I put the 328 in first gear and left Griswold's house behind. I was in no hurry to tell Fleener or Hendricks they oughta arrest the whole wacky bunch. Just because.

I decided to take M-119 out of Cross Village. I remember when no one called it the "Tunnel of Trees," when it was just a very curvy stretch of blacktop down to Harbor Springs. In those years, the road was dotted with small clapboard houses, often in need of fresh white paint or a new roof. Most of the residents were second or third generation families deeply rooted in rural Northern Michigan. Not anymore. The new McMansions were fashionable summer playpens of the rich. They were often built on property where two frame houses once stood. No fieldstone wall protected the owners, but were these folks any different than Wardcliff and Nickelson?

I'd just pulled into a parking space next to the New York Restaurant when my phone chirped. I picked it up and swiped the glass, "Michael Russo."

Nothing for a second. "Russo," I said again.

"This Michael Russo?" a man's voice said.

"Yeah. Who's this?"

"This is a friend," the voice said. "Be a good time to forget Cherokee Point."

I hung up. I checked the number. A 317 area code. Indiana? I wanted a bowl of soup, maybe a beer. Before I could get out of the car, the phone chirped again. Same number. "How'd you get this number?"

"Never hang up on me again, got it?"

"Don't tell me your name. Don't tell me why you're calling. Or where you are. But you threaten me? Fuck off." Click. I moved the switch to vibrate and dropped the phone on the seat. Now it was a beer, for sure, then the soup. I left the car and went into the restaurant.

Twenty minutes later, with a tasty bowel of split pea and a Beck's under my belt, I got back in the car for the ride to the office. I checked the phone. No more calls.

I parked at my apartment building, walked down Bay Street and cut across the parking lot behind the office. Sandy had that look on her face when I walked in. "What?" I said, almost smirking. She pointed at my office and shook her head.

Martin Fleener was planted in the chair behind my desk. "Trying it on for size?" I said. "In case you retire early?"

"Might be forced retirement you keep screwing around," he said. "What the hell did you do out there, anyway?"

"Don't yell at me, Marty. I just spent an hour on an Antebellum plantation. I've been treated like an idiot, treated like a child and then threatened. I don't need you on my case."

"Threatened?"

"Besides, you got me into this." I sat down in the chair opposite my desk.

"You want your chair?" Fleener asked. I shook my head. I saw Sandy at the door. I waved my arm. "You might as well sit down, too." She did, in the chair next to mine. "I haven't been gone that long, yet here you are, waiting for me. What put a burr up your ass?"

"What happened out there, Michael? I get this call from Fishers, Indiana, wherever the hell that is. Senator Harrison's Chief of Staff said you picked a fight out there as soon as you walked in the door. Then said you told him to and I quote, 'fuck off.' That was after you hung up on him the first time."

"Did all that in just a couple of hours?" Sandy said, like I'd just won a prize. "You da man!"

Fleener looked over at Sandy. "You're a big help," he said. "The Senator's not happy, Hendricks' is not happy, I'm not happy. Tell me."

I told them about my morning at Cherokee Point. "Had a good run, though."

"Shut up," Fleener said with no inflection. "You sure Harrison's COS never identified himself?" I shook my head slowly. "Either time?" Shook my head again.

"He called you?" I asked.

"After he called Hendricks." Fleener stood up, walked to the window, turned around and leaned back against the casing. "Also wanted to know why you accused Griswold and Abbott of being mobbed up."

"The Mafia? Woo, hoo," Sandy said, with a grin on her face. "Getting better all the time."

Fleener looked over at Sandy. Again without inflection he said, "Shut up."

"Never said anything about the Mafia."

"Say anything about Joey D. or Carmine?"

"Threw in their names."

Fleener came off the window. "Jesus, Russo."

"Didn't accuse anybody of anything, Marty. Just wanted to see if the names got a reaction."

Fleener sat back down in my chair. "Well, you got a reaction, all right. We send you out there to get their cooperation…"

I put my hands in the air, palms up. "Hey, Marty."

"I know, I know," he said.

"You holding out on me?"

"No more than usual," he said.

"Is there more to the DeMio connection? Are father and son more involved with Nick than we think?"

"Joey runs the show, Michael. Carmine's really retired."

"Be good to talk to Carmine first," I said. "Not Joey. Respect for the father. See what his kid's up to at Cherokee Point."

Fleener leaned forward, elbows on the desk. "Maybe you should, Michael. Maybe you should."

"More here than we think," I said.

Sandy clapped her hands. Caught us by surprise. "Yahoo! The mob, the Point, now, Mackinac Island. Doesn't get any better than this." Fleener and I both glared at her.

Fleener turned back to me. "We're missing something, Michael."

9

"**F**leener's right." Hendricks dropped both feet off his desk with a thud. He turned and looked at the window behind the desk. "Can't open the damn thing," he said. "Nice day like this." He loosened his tie as he glanced at me. "Your office window open?" I nodded. "Your goddamn building's seventy, eighty years old. The window works?"

"Fixed it when I bought the building, Don."

Hendricks scratched a spot behind his left ear. "Want more coffee?" I shook my head. My caffeine buzz was headed for the redline. "What are we missing, Michael?"

"You're the prosecutor," I said. "Who's suspect number one?"

"Nickelson Abbott," he said. "Like I said before, family first."

"Motive?"

"Money and lots of it," he said.

"Parker?"

"Don't think so," Hendricks said. "We'll keep digging, but…" he shrugged. "We confirmed that Nick gets Carleton's business, his money and the property at the Point."

"Think I said that." He ignored me. "You gonna bring Nick in for questioning?"

Hendricks nodded. "Just not sure how to do it."

"How about handcuffs and a cop car?"

"Michael . . ."

"Sorry," I said. "Maybe you oughta ask the Senator or the Congressman to, ah, encourage Nick to come to your office."

"Talked about that," he said. "Probably what we do."

"Might set an example for the boys at the Point. Doing their civic duty and all, just like good ole Nick."

"It might," Hendricks said, "it just might."

"Can I sit in on the interview when you get him here?" I said.

"From behind the glass. Not in the room." Hendricks looked at his watch. "Gotta go, Michael. Staff meeting in a few minutes." Hendricks got out of his chair. "Have to get that window fixed," he said. He walked around the desk and headed for the door.

"Give me call," I said.

I went down Division to Lake Street and turned towards the office. Until Hendricks got Nick Abbott in for questions, I had nowhere to go but Mackinac Island. Nobody at Cherokee Point would talk to me, so visiting Carmine DeMio was the only plan I had. Mentioning DeMio's name got a reaction. Maybe actually talking to him would stir things up.

I stuck my head in the door at Mackinac Sandal Company. "Hi, Janet," I said. Janet Tarvis, a twenty-four-year-old retailing graduate from Central Michigan, managed the shoe store for Fran Warren. "Fran around?"

"Hey, Michael. She's at Roast & Toast," Tarvis said, pointing her finger towards the coffee shop four doors away.

I walked down the street.

Fran was reading the paper and drinking coffee at a two-top by the wall. "Can I join you?" I asked.

"Michael, what a nice surprise. Please do," she said, gesturing at the chair. She folded up her newspaper as I sat down.

"Fran, can I tap your brain about the Island?"

"Of course," she said.

"Thought I'd call on Carmine DeMio," I said.

"Do I look like his secretary?"

"Very funny," I said. "You know where he hangs out? Who he spends time with? That kind of thing."

"If he comes to town," she said, "it's the dining room or the bar at the Marquette Park Hotel. You know it?"

I nodded. "Walked by often enough. Never been inside. You like the place?"

"Beautiful hotel. One of the oldest buildings on the Island. Completely restored. Meet friends at the bar, mostly."

"Any place else?" I said.

Fran shook her head. "He owns the hotel. Got an office, too. Word is he feels safe there." Warren got up. "Refill my coffee. Want something?"

"No thanks," I said. I picked up her copy of *The New York Times*. Front page story on Hillary Clinton's likely run for president. Wonder how many afternoons were ruined at Cherokee Point when they got the news?

Fran sat down. "Call DeMio's house. Number's in the book. He really does have a secretary. Guy named Vollini. Big. Looks tough." Fran drank her coffee. "Michael," she said. "Talk is you're playing cop. That true?"

"Told Don Hendricks I'd help him out. That's all."

"That's all?" she said. "Rumor has it you got into trouble pretty fast." I shrugged.

"Don't mess with these guys, Michael," Fran said. "They're not nice people. You'll get more than a cold shoulder from them."

10

I got to A.J.'s house shortly after six. She lives up Bay Street from my office in a stately two-story Victorian. White with gray-blue trim. She's been remodeling it room by room for more than five years. Started with structural updates, insulation, heating, roof. Then it was on to paint, inside and out. It looked much like it must have when it was built eighty years ago.

"Darling," she said, as I put my brief bag at the door and stepped into the kitchen. "How's about a big hug?"

"You bet." I put my arms around her waist and pulled her to me. Tight. We kissed, slowly, softly at first, then harder. "You feel wonderful," I said, stepping back. "You look pretty good, too."

"In this ole thing," she said, badly imitating a Southern Belle. "Why, honey chile, it's just a pair of tight shorts and a loose, floppy top with some buttons open."

"Uh-huh," I said. "You look good enough to eat. But I see a couple of Caprese salads and a French baguette over there." I nodded towards the small table next to a kitchen window. "Any Chardonnay around?"

A.J. opened the refrigerator door and pulled out a nicely chilled bottle. "You do the honors," she said.

We ate quietly for a few minutes, enjoying the moment of being together.

"How did it go with Hendricks?" she asked. I told her. Told her about Fleener's comments, too. "You think all of you are missing something?"

I nodded. "Not many players to keep track of. Nick Abbott and Parker Abbott are about it. Right? Nick's got the motive. Not sure about opportunity."

"Works if Nick's got no alibi." A.J. cocked her head and turned her palms up. "But if he does, then what?"

We put our plates in the sink, poured more wine and went to the living room couch. I sat back, put my feet on the coffee table. "I'm not sure where to go with it if Nick's clean."

"You going to the Island to see Carmine DeMio?"

I nodded.

"Then it's obvious."

"What's obvious?" I said.

"Some lawyer you are. Remind me never to hire you for anything important."

"Smart-ass. What's your point?"

"Who's the only other person with an unhealthy connection to both Nick and Parker?"

"Joey D.," I said.

"Yes, Joey D."

"You think Joey killed Carleton Abbott?"

"Could be," A.J. said.

"But Nick's gambling losses and drug buys are small change for a Chicago wiseguy."

"Unless Abbott's death means even bigger bucks for Joey."

I got off the couch and went for more wine. "Want some?"

A.J. shook her head. I filled my glass and put it on the coffee table. I walked to the window and looked out over the ravine behind the house. Middle of town, but it's all trees and hills. I turned around, put my hands on my hips and said, "Think Joey killed Abbott?"

A.J. nodded.

"Cops finger Nick because he owed the bad guys lots of money?"

She nodded again.

"Nick does hard time and Joey D. cuddles up with Parker and the money?"

A.J. nodded, slowly. "Keep thinking smart. I might just take you to my bed and screw your lights out."

"I love it when you use subtlety to seduce me."

"Subtlety? Let's go," she said, gesturing at the bedroom.

My cell chimed. I looked at A.J.

"Read it," she said. "I'm not going anywhere. Gotta get out of these damn shorts. Too tight."

"Fleener's bringing Nick in for questioning. Nine tomorrow."

"Then we got plenty of time," she said. "Get your clothes off."

"That more subtlety at work?"

"Get in here, will ya. I'm about to be very unsubtle."

11

Nickelson Abbott sat quietly in a metal chair, his hands folded neatly on the edge of the gray metal table. The scowl on his face was noticeable, but he looked every bit the social aristocrat he wanted to be. A navy doubled-breasted blazer covered a soft red polo shirt above a pair of perfectly creased summer weight gray wool slacks. Natty for the boardroom or the country club dining room.

Next to him sat Jason Richardson, criminal defense specialist from Detroit. Richardson's thirty-year career on behalf of several of the Motor City's most notorious mob figures made him well known to law enforcement agencies in the Great Lakes states.

Across the table sat Captain Martin Fleener. A stenographer chewed gum quietly in the corner with her machine. Don Hendricks and I watched through the window. Behind us stood a uniformed officer.

"Mr. Abbott," Fleener started, "thank you for coming in today."

"You can take your thank you and . . ." Abbott said, but Richardson's hand shot out from under the table and grabbed his arm.

"We hope that we can resolve Mr. Abbott's problems today, sir," Richardson said in a subdued voice. "Mr. Abbott wants nothing more than to cooperate with the police so that he and his sister are free to grieve the loss of their father." Richardson reached for his briefcase and took out some papers. "It is obvious to me that the heinous murder of Carleton Abbott was a random act of violence, uncommon at Cherokee Point."

"Random, my ass," I said on the other side of the glass. "Does he actually expect anyone to believe that?"

"Shut up," Hendricks said. "Doesn't expect anything. He's trying to figure out what we got."

"Have any more than you told me?" I said.

"No."

Fleener leaned back in his chair, its front feet off the floor. His hands rested on the edge of the table. "We, too, want to resolve several things about the death of Mr. Abbott," he said. "Let's begin with the week before the murder."

For almost two hours, the questions came; about Nickelson, about Parker, about the family, about the Point.

I said, "We're not getting anywhere." I looked down at my mug. "Except I don't think I'll ever want your coffee again."

"Thought you were smart, Russo." Hendricks said. "It's more than Nick. We want the other gentlemen of Cherokee Point in here. Never know what we might find out."

When it seemed that Fleener was almost finished, Richardson asked for a moment. He got up and Abbott followed him to a corner of the room.

I looked over at Hendricks. He shrugged and shook his head. We waited.

Both men returned to the table.

"Captain," Richardson said. "Gentlemen," he said, gesturing at the mirror, "Mr. Abbott would like to make a statement. We've discussed the issue and I concur that it is in the best interests of Cherokee Point and Mr. Abbott to convey certain details about the night of the murder."

Whoa. Got my attention. Hendricks put down his coffee and turned up the volume.

"Captain," Abbott said. "On the night of my father's brutal death, I was in Cheboygan, at a private home. All night."

"All night?" Fleener asked.

Abbott nodded.

"What time did you arrive in Cheboygan?"

"Late afternoon. Maybe four, four-thirty."

"You left at what time?"

"The next morning. Probably seven."

"Do you have any witnesses to your out of town visit?" Fleener said.

With that, Richardson opened his briefcase, pulled out a single sheet of paper and slid it across the table. "This is a signed affidavit from one Irene Castle of Cheboygan, Michigan. She'll confirm that Mr. Abbott spent the entire evening in question at her house."

"Well, shit," Hendricks said.

"Yep," I said.

Richardson took out a small spiral notebook, wrote something and tore off a page. "Here," he said, handing the small sheet to Fleener. "Ms. Castle's cell. Be discreet. She's married and only agreed to help Mr. Abbott to prevent a miscarriage of justice."

"When pigs fly." Hendricks said. He looked over his shoulder. "Officer."

"Yes, sir." The officer left the room and moments later entered the interrogation room. Fleener handed the officer the paper. Richardson turned his head towards the mirror, towards us and smiled.

When the officer reappeared at the door, Hendricks said, "Give it to Lt. Fawcett."

"It'll check out, you know," I said.

"Of course, it will," Hendricks said.

"You wonder how Nick just happened to be represented by a mob lawyer?" I said.

"DeMio."

"Could be a coincidence."

Hendricks shot me a look. "You believe in coincidences?"

I shook my head. "Who tops the list now? Parker or Joey D?"

"Not Parker. When you going to Mackinac Island?"

"Sandy'll call for an appointment," I said. "I'll let you know." I picked up my brief bag and hung it on my right shoulder. "Can you email me the Lansing file on DeMio, father and son?"

Hendricks shook his head. "Classified. They'd have my ass if I did that." He paused for a moment. "What I can do," he said, "is write up basic information on the DeMios and send that. Sound okay?"

I nodded and went for the door.

"Michael," Hendricks said. I looked back. "Thought we'd only get the clowns at Cherokee Point. Didn't see any heavy hitters in this game."

I nodded. "Haven't been to the Island since last fall, Don," I said. "Time I went. Clouds, rain, cold wind off the water. What's not to love?"

"Yeah," Hendricks said. He turned back towards the glass. "Keep in touch."

12

"I talked with Carmine DeMio's, ah. . ." Sandy said, ". . .secretary? His scheduler? His whatever? Guy sounded like he smoked two packs a day since he was five."

"And?"

"Got you an appointment for the day after tomorrow. Dining room at the Marquette Park Hotel at ten for breakfast."

"Thanks," I said.

I sat at my desk and sifted through my messages. Nothing urgent, but I still needed clients to pay the bills. Jane Friedman's farmhouse got a clean inspection report, so I could schedule the closing. Nothing new on the Savage divorce.

My phone chimed. A.J. wanted to meet for a drink at City Park Grill, then home for dinner. I tapped "yes."

"Michael," Sandy said from the doorway, "there's a Mr. Sheridan to see you." Then in a whisper, "no appointment."

"Send him in." I stood up and came around the desk. In walked a man in his late thirties, nice looking with a square jaw, short dark hair, a bright smile, stylish glasses. He wore navy shorts, an apple green polo shirt and brown Birkenstocks. Wonder if he got 'em downstairs.

He reached out and we shook hands. "Good to meet you," Sheridan said.

"Sit down, please," I said, gesturing at the chair opposite my desk. "Would you like something? Coffee, water?"

"No thank you, Mr. Russo."

"Call me Michael," I said. "It's Kelsey, isn't it?" He nodded. "What can I do for you?"

"I'm not sure what you know about me, but I might be able to help you."

I opened the police file on the Abbott case, flipped through several pages. "Let's see, you're thirty-eight . . ."

"Thirty-nine."

"Thirty-nine, live in Bloomfield Hills . . ."

"The old, original part," he said.

I nodded. "Been coming to Cherokee Point all your life. Dartmouth grad. Doesn't say what in." I looked up.

"Creative Writing," he said.

"How's the job market?"

"Not so hot. Especially here," he said, with a slow wave of the hand.

"Better in Birmingham?"

"Not enough better."

I nodded. "And you're the lucky man who found Carleton Abbott," I said and closed the file.

"That's one way to look at it," he said.

Sharp guy. "Tell me about finding Abbott."

He did. "I've never seen a dead person before."

"How'd you know he was dead?"

"I just knew, that's all," he said. "The way his arm was tangled in the net." Kelsey shook his head slowly and looked down at his lap. "I just knew."

"And you called the cops?"

Kelsey nodded. "I stayed there until they arrived." He hesitated. "But not near the body. Couldn't do that."

I waited for a moment to let him collect his thoughts and himself. "What can I do for you?"

"Mr. Russo, ah, Michael, I think I can help with your case."

"Carleton Abbott?" I said.

He nodded.

"The case belongs to the police, Kelsey, not me."

"Mr. Russo, everybody knows what you're doing. Give me five minutes. Listen to what I have to say. You think I'm out of line, I'll apologize for taking up your time and be on my way."

"Okay," I said, "take your time."

"I want to be a writer. Mystery novels. I've read all the best. Hammett, Chandler, of an earlier time. Parker, Hamilton, Crais. I learn from them. How to write, I hope. How to build a story." I shifted in my chair. I wanted to turn around and look at the bay. But I didn't want to be rude.

"How's your passion for mysteries help here?"

"I have a theory of the case," he said. "Willing to listen?" I nodded. "This is not a random killing. Way I see it, you got three suspects. All connected to Cherokee Point." He was off to a good start, but that's all it was, a start.

"Nick Abbott, Parker Abbott, Joey DeMio. If I were writing a mystery about the Abbott killing, they'd be the only suspects. Murder is about money, sex or revenge. Agreed?"

"Pretty much," I said.

"Take Nick. No motive." Sheridan leaned forward in the chair and clasped his hands in front of him. "Nick will get all his father's money, the Cherokee Point property and his business interests. He buys drugs from DeMio. He's been gambling since he could reach up and slap a chip on the table. Sex? Rumor has it he's had several women on the side. His wife doesn't seem to care, so that leaves revenge. Against whom? For what? Not clear to me, anyway." I listened, but hadn't heard anything helpful.

"Next would be Joey DeMio. Joey D. The man. Obvious choice. Mafia killer, right? Money? He gets money from lots of people, including Nick. Sex? Plenty of that, too, from Parker. Probably others. Revenge? Nothing. If anybody wanted to get even, it was Carleton Abbott. Shoudda shot Joey D. for screwing his daughter. That didn't happen, of course."

Sheridan got out of his chair slowly, almost thoughtfully, and walked to the window. "Nice view," he said. "I love Northern Michigan, I really do. Always felt my heart was here." He turned towards me and put his hands in his pockets. "Believe it or not, I love Cherokee Point, too. The place, anyway. The people? Most of them, I've known all my life. Never understood the fanatic need for privacy. From whom? Locals? Why?" Sheridan walked back around the desk. He put both arms out and leaned on the back of the chair. "Would Cherokee Point evaporate tomorrow without the uber-privacy? Give me a break. They could use a good dose of reality. You know, how the 'other half' lives." He made quote signs with his fingers in the air.

"You got that dose of reality, Kelsey?" I said. "At Dartmouth?"

"Of course not," he said. "Don't patronize me, Mr. Russo. I've lived an easy life. Still do, or I'd be working at Wal-Mart right now. But at least I let the outside air into my system, which is more than I can say for the ladies and gentlemen at Cherokee Point." The "ladies and gentlemen" had an edge to it. Came out through clenched teeth.

"I apologize, Kelsey," I said.

"Apology accepted." He sat in the chair. "Your killer is Parker Abbott."

"Because?"

"Two out of three. Revenge mostly, then money. In that order, but they're bound together." Kelsey Sheridan had my attention now.

"I'm listening."

"Parker hated her father."

"Really," I said, "you know this how?"

"Known her all my life. She's always been on the Point. Leaves for a job someplace. California, Florida, whatever. But it never worked out. Always came back. Lives at the cottage. Can't seem to make it anywhere else."

"Let me ask you something, Kelsey," I said, "don't you think that's a lot of guesswork on your part?"

"Obvious question. But at Cherokee Point, everyone pays attention to everyone else's business. There's an old saw on the Point. Goes something like this, Want to keep something quiet, don't even tell me. Over the years, I listen. To my parents, my parents' friends, my friends. Listen enough for long enough and you get a pretty good picture of what people are doing."

"Back to Parker," I said.

"She hated her father. He aced her out of the estate. Nick was the favorite because Nick was a male. Men rule at Cherokee Point. Nick inherits everything. Parker remains a second-class citizen. Nick replaces their father as the big man. She'll have to beg her brother for money. Nick will be nastier to his sister than her father ever was. Sibling rivalry gone wild."

"Killing her father doesn't get her the estate."

"It does if Nick lands in jail for killing their father."

"Why would Nick kill his father if he gets the estate anyway?"

"To get it faster. Remember, Nick's in hock to Joey D. for the gambling losses. Mob killers are not patient people."

Sheridan and Hendricks seemed to have reached similar conclusions. No secrets and lots of gossip at Cherokee Point.

"Falls flat if Nick's cleared," I said, knowing that he had been.

"Sure," Sheridan said. "Then Joey D. moves to the top of the list. You think Parker hops into bed with him because he's the apple of her eye? Because she hopes to be 'Mrs. Joseph DeMio,' princess of Mafia land?"

I shrugged.

"Parker uses sex to keep him around. Next thing you know, cops think Joey bumped off old man Abbott so Nick will get the money to pay off his debt and buy more drugs. Parker plants the idea of a conspiracy to kill Abbott. Pillow talk, you know. Nick and Joey land in jail and she takes over."

"You really think so," I said.

Sheridan nodded. "That's the way I'd write it."

"Due respect?" I said.

"Of course."

"Great theory for a mystery novel, but not real life," I said. "Nick's the obvious choice for several reasons and you mentioned most of them. If Nick's got an alibi, the cops might look at DeMio. But they're not interested in Parker. No solid motive for killing her father."

Sheridan sat for a minute and said nothing. "Hate so strong it leads to murder? Maybe the hate's built on more than money," he said. "But you're right. Too complicated. Never happen in real life."

Sheridan stood and reached out his hand. "It was good to meet you," he said. We shook hands. "Good to meet the man who annoyed two of Cherokee Point's poobahs in one brief meeting."

"Not one of my better days," I said.

"No? You dropped Joey DeMio's name. Things heated up fast after that, didn't they?"

I must have looked surprised.

"Cops'll be hot for Joey. Solves everybody's problem. One nice package. A good day to you, Mr. Russo," Kelsey Sheridan said.

"And to you, Kelsey." I watched him leave the office and wondered about that last remark.

13

The City Park Grill sits at the edge of Pennsylvania Park, up Lake Street from my office. Ernest Hemingway often used a stool at one end of the solid mahogany bar to think up new stories. The original iteration of the Grill in the 1880s only served men. A.J. always found that amusing as she sipped a nice Chardonnay. "Progress," she said sarcastically, "progress."

I spotted A.J. at Hemingway's end of the bar. She sat with her boss, Maury Weston, publisher of the *Petoskey Post Dispatch*. Weston took over as publisher in 2001 after a long career at the paper as a general news reporter, then editor, shortly after graduation from Michigan State. His lean, six-six-frame commanded attention when he entered a room, just as it did when he walked on the Jenison Fieldhouse basketball floor for the Spartans in the mid-1970s.

Weston saw me first and waved. I made my way over and we shook hands. "How are you, Maury?" I said.

"Good, Michael. Thanks for asking."

I sat down on the stool next to A.J. "A good looking sweater you got there, my friend," I said to Weston. He wore gray worsted slacks and a light blue button down, open at the collar, under a cashmere sweater with soft red and blue stripes.

"Thanks," he said. "Everyone wants casual these days. Decided not to fight it any longer. Created standards for casual dress instead."

"The staff does look pretty sharp," A.J. said.

"Have you two solved all the woes of modern journalism?" I said.

Weston laughed. "If we could do that, we'd be in New York making really big bucks."

"Yes, we would," A.J. said emphatically and raised her glass. "I'd be thinking about which Broadway play I'd see tonight. Instead, it'll be a hot bath and into bed."

"Actually, we are making progress on *PPD Wired* thanks to A.J.'s hard work," Weston said, nodding in her direction. "But she can fill you in on the details." He lifted himself off the stool. "Time for me to head home." Weston said his good-byes and left the restaurant.

"Want to eat at the bar?" A.J. asked. "We can eat home another night."

"Sure."

"Something to drink, Mr. Russo?" Meg asked. Margaret Samuels was twenty-something, five-two, with shoulder length brown hair. The newest member of the Grill staff came from Houghton-Hancock, in the UP, she told us one night. Wanted to live in the "big city" she said.

"An Oban on the rocks," I said. A.J. lifted her nearly empty wine glass by the stem.

The bartender put menus in front of us. "One special tonight," she said. "Chopped sirloin with choice of potato and vegetable. Comes with a small tossed salad. Back in a few."

"Maury seems optimistic about *PPD Wired*. You feel better about it?"

"In a word, yes," A.J. said. "Maury gave me plenty of rope to get the job done or hang myself," she said and started to laugh. "It was such a mess when I took over. Weston's a guy who focused on local news when few others did. Way ahead of his time. When the internet stole the national news, he was positioned to lead our paper back to the era of local news and made money doing it."

Meg put drinks in front of us. "Ready to order?"

"I'll have the chopped sirloin special," I said, "baked potato, ranch on the salad." A.J. ordered a whitefish sandwich with fries.

"As sharp as Maury was about the future of print journalism, he dropped the ball on the electronic edition."

"Savvy enough to pick you to fix it," I said.

"Hope so," she said. "Anything new with your case?"

"That's the second time today someone's called it 'my case.' Wish people'd stop doing that."

"For Pete's sake, Michael, everyone knows what you're doing."

"Second time for that line, too."

"Bag the critique and update me. Leave more time later to discuss your body parts," she said and smiled.

I told her about Kelsey Sheridan's visit and his storyline for the Abbott murder.

"I don't get his DeMio comment."

"Me either," I said, "but it caught me."

"Think he was trying to tell you something?"

"Maybe. Pretty vague for a guy who just spelled out his pet theory in detail."

"Parker?"

"Uh-huh."

"Think she killed her father?"

"No," I said. "It just doesn't add up. Wish it did. I could finish this thing and spend more time with you. Or my paying clients."

"Thanks for lumping me together with divorcees and deadbeats."

"Hush. You know what I mean."

Meg arrived with two plates of hot food followed by the appropriate condiments.

"Thanks, Meg," A.J. said.

"My pleasure. Enjoy."

A.J. bit into her sandwich. "Hmm. Tasty." After a moment, she swallowed some wine. "Got an idea, Michael."

"For sex?"

"That's for later, darling. Worth the wait," she said. "Suppose Joey DeMio is involved."

"He's about to be brought in for questioning. That involved enough?"

"Yeah," A.J. said, "but not because he's a suspect."

"As what, then?"

"A red herring, darling," she said. "Remember Kelsey Sheridan's scenario."

"Meg," I said. The bartender looked my way. I put two fingers in the air and she nodded. "Think DeMio's a misdirection?"

"I do," she said. She picked up another French fry, pointed it at me before putting it her mouth. "That's what Kelsey was telling you."

"That Joey's the wrong guy?"

"Yes. I mean, no." A.J. turned sideways on the barstool and put her hand on my arm. "Look, Joey's the wrong man for the murder but the right man to pin it on."

"Really?"

A.J. nodded. "If Nick's in the clear. The obvious next choice is DeMio. Soon as the Mafia guy's 'numero uno,' everyone gets on board."

"I really want to kiss you right now," I said.

"Make it quick. I'm not done." I kissed her. She kissed me back. "It's so easy to make Joey the killer. Cops rid the community of a dreaded bad guy, Cherokee Point goes back to sleep, you resume fantasizing about me."

"I dunno," I said, shaking my head. I sipped my scotch, then cut off a piece of chopped steak.

"Even you think he's the guy," A.J. said. "It gets everybody off the hook. That's what Kelsey meant."

Meg Samuels picked up our plates. "Anything else?" she asked.

"We're done, Meg," A.J. said. "Just the check, please."

"Okay, so we're all off the hook, as you put it. Right?"

A.J. nodded.

"To what end?"

"The red herring makes it easier for the killer to hide."

"Parker?"

"Parker."

I looked at the tab and put cash on the bar. "Thanks, Meg," I said and waved in her direction.

We left the City Park Grill and walked down Lake Street.

"Keep throwing greenbacks around. Makes me hot for your body."

"You're already hot for my body," I said.

"More heat never hurts."

"True." I put my arm around her waist as we walked. "A long night of hot sex before my showdown with the Mafia on Mackinac Island."

"You are so melodramatic, sometimes."

14

The afternoon sun hung over Little Traverse Bay as I eased the 328 into gear and headed up U.S. 31 for the forty-five minute ride to Mackinaw City.

I was four-years old when I first set foot on Mackinac Island. Don't remember much about that trip, but I remember most of them since. Summer after summer, weekend after weekend, vacation after vacation, Mackinac Island infected my imagination and my heart. The "land of the great turtle" was first the land of the French, then the British, always Native American and now a summer colony of tourists and residents in a curious mix of history, commerce and fun.

I never tire of pulling into the harbor and taking in the expanse of the downtown, Fort Mackinac and the bluff cottages. In one of those cottages on the East Bluff lived Carmine DeMio. I decided not to plan for the meeting, instead to let DeMio give me whatever he wanted to give.

I caught the five o'clock ferry and stepped on the dock fifteen minutes later. I picked up my bag, slung it over my shoulder and walked up Hoban Street to the Cloghaun. The bed and breakfast sat at the top of the street. A two-story Victorian decked out in white paint, a central stairway to the double front door and an eye-catching array of flowers, plants and shrubs. Sandy'd booked me in the only room with a private entrance. She reminded me that it was nicknamed, "the love and lust room" because honeymooners always wanted to reserve it. I wish. Love probably wouldn't be DeMio's first reaction when he heard his kid's up to bat against the cops.

The Cloghaun was comfortable, charmingly filled with American antiques and a short walk down Market Street from the Marquette

Park Hotel where I hoped breakfast with Carmine DeMio would add something to what little I knew about the killer of Carleton Abbott. So far Kelsey Sheridan and A.J. were on the right track. Nick Abbott was accused then cleared, now Joey DeMio was accused.

"Welcome, Mr. Russo," said a tall, attractive woman in her twenties. She had brown hair pulled back and held in place by an enormous purple plastic clip. "You'll be with us for one night?"

"Correct," I said.

"You've already paid," she said, looking at the screen. "And the notation says you've stayed with us before."

"I have." She handed me the key. I told her I knew the way to my room.

"Very good," she said. "Enjoy your visit to Mackinac Island."

I opened my bag on the bed and took out a pair of khaki shorts and a long-sleeve green T-shirt that said "Lilac Festival 10K, 2008" across the front. I switched clothes, happily leaving behind my street gear. I slipped on my Chaco sandals, grabbed the key and headed downtown.

I walked down "Back Street," a calmer and more peaceful avenue than Main Street as the tourist season swung into gear. A couple of men hammered away at the stairs at City Hall and the Post Office fence was getting a new coat of white paint. I crossed Fort Street and walked into Marquette Park.

Carmine DeMio's Marquette Park Hotel stood at the other end of the large open space. Built before the Civil War as a private estate, the hotel passed through several owners before DeMio bought it in 1998. Like most old buildings in the harsh environment of Northern Michigan, the four-story hotel with the white façade had undergone constant renovation and repair.

I sat down on the cement wall at the base of the park. Over the years, I've spent a lot of time sitting on this wall, watching the world of Mackinac Island go by on Main Street. Dock porters and drays, taxis and tourists. Watched a few Lilac Festival parades from right here, too.

I felt like the hotel was looming over my shoulder. It wasn't dread, exactly. Of course, I've never talked with a real Mafioso before and this is a murder investigation, after all. Maybe I'd seen *The Godfather* too many times.

15

I stayed on the wall for a time. Liked being back on the Island, but I was ready for a burger and beer at the Mustang. I wanted to be up early to get a long morning run in before meeting DeMio.

I walked down Main Street to Astor Street and turned the corner. The Mackinac Sandal Company was crowded with business when I looked in the door. Fran Warren always insisted that the Island store was easier for customers to find than her Petoskey store because everyone knew the Mustang. Much as I wanted to say hello to Fran, I walked across the street to the Mustang instead.

I took a stool at the bar. "What can I get you?" said the bartender, a guy with a buzz cut and wire-rimmed glasses. He looked too young to be in a bar, let alone work in one.

"A draft, please," I said, "and a menu."

"You got it," he said, pointing his finger, pistol style, my way. A coaster, the beer and the menu landed in front of me. "Holler when you're ready to order."

"Will do," I said, pointing my finger pistol back at him.

Only a few tables were busy, but it was early. Mostly tourists. A scruffy looking guy in a baggy black sweatshirt nursed a beer at the far end of the bar. He'd been here for a while.

The beer tasted good. Over one corner of the bar a large TV played ESPN. Soccer. I enjoyed the beer more.

I gave serious thought to ordering another one when a guy sat down next to me and almost knocked me off my stool. I looked to my right. His face—big, round, puffy with a red nose—stared right at me. "Sorry, pal," he said, dragging out the word, "pal."

Before I could say anything, I got pushed hard from the other side into Mr. Red Nose on my right. "Hey, watch out," he said and shoved me back into the new guy on my left.

"Well, excuse me, buddy," Mr. Lefty said. He was just as tall as the other man, but with a chiseled face, dark skin and a small goatee. Being the crack investigator that I am, I concluded that the arrival of these two guys was no coincidence.

"Lotta rude people in the world. Ain't that right, Gino?" It was Mr. Lefty.

"Yeah," Mr. Red Nose said. "Whaddya have to do to get a beer around here?" The bartender, so punctual in my case, was nowhere in sight. Another coincidence?

"Beats me," said Mr. Lefty. I was being squeezed hard between the two of them. My pleasant evening had taken a decidedly sour turn.

"Gentlemen," I said, as friendly as I could. "I'd be glad to swap stools, so you two can continue your conversation."

"Well, goddamn, Santino," Mr. Red Nose said, "can ya beat this guy? Try to be nice and whadda we get? Maybe we oughta teach him . . ."

Caught it out of the corner of my eye. Something moved. Fast. Mr. Red Nose never finished his sentence. He was on the floor, looking every bit like a beached whale, staring up at a man standing next to me. The man was six-three, a trained 230, the muscles in his chest and arms barely concealed by a navy T-shirt. He wore baggy gray shorts and dirty Brooks running shoes. "Terribly sorry, sir," he said. "May I help you up?" No one in the bar moved.

Mr. Lefty, Santino, came off his stool. He'd taken only one step when the stranger spun around and put his arm straight out, palm up, traffic cop style. Santino froze. The hand in the air turned into a finger pistol. The stranger's finger slowly turned and pointed at the door. Santino's eyes followed. So did mine. Leaning against the wall was a Mackinac Island police officer. Blue uniform with his arms crossed over his chest. And armed.

"Officer Concannon," the stranger said, "don't you think it's a shame this man can't enjoy his beer in peace and quiet?"

"Yes, I do," the officer said. Concannon left the wall and walked to the bar. He looked at Santino, still standing and Gino, still on the floor. "Gentlemen," he said. "Would you be so kind as to allow this paying customer," he gestured in my direction, "to savor his beer?" He put his hands on his hips, one hand rested on the handle of his pistol. "Alone."

"Santino stood still.

"Get up," Officer Concannon said sharply, gesturing at Gino. "Slowly."

Gino raised himself to one knee, then all the way up. "That's good," he said. "Enjoy the sights, gentlemen." He looked at Santino, who hesitated for a moment, then started for the door. Gino followed. I watched them walk towards Main Street. People in the Mustang began to move again.

"Thank you," I said, looking first at the stranger then at the officer. I extended my hand to the stranger. "Michael Russo," I said.

"I know," he said as we shook hands. "Henri LaCroix. Glad to meet you."

"And thank you, as well, Officer," I said, and we shook hands.

I turned back to LaCroix. "Have we met before?" I said.

He shook his head, but pointed outside, through the window, using a finger pistol. Must be a genetic trait on Mackinac.

I looked out the window and across the street stood Fran Warren at the door of the Sandal Company. She smiled, waved vigorously and started towards the bar. A moment later, she came through the door.

"Good evening, Michael," she said, "I see you've met Mr. LaCroix and Officer William Concannon." The two men greeted Fran.

"I have," I said, hesitating. "What was all this?" I asked gesturing vaguely in front of me.

"Saw you walk in from my window," Warren said, pointing over her shoulder at the Sandal Company. "Didn't think anything of it until DeMio's goons came up the street."

"Those guys work for Carmine DeMio?"

"They do," Officer Concannon said. "Santino Cicci and Gino Rosato. If DeMio's on the island, they're on the island. And, now, if you'll excuse me, I'll be on my way."

"Thank you, again," I said. Officer Concannon nodded and left the bar.

"Let's sit down," Fran Warren said, and we took a table by the back wall.

The bartender reappeared and put a fresh beer in front of me. "On the house," he said.

"Getcha some food?"

"Burger deluxe, medium, with fries," I said.

"Be up in a minute. Get you anything, Fran, Henri?"

"Warren shook her head. "Still working."

"Well, I'm not," LaCroix said, "I'll have a draft, too."

"Let me get this straight," I said to Fran. "You thought I'd have trouble with those guys, so you called your friends?"

"Oh, I knew you'd have trouble. Only question was when."

The bartender set my burger on the table and put a beer down for LaCroix. "Enjoy," he said, without activating the finger pistol.

"I asked Henri to keep an eye on you," Warren said.

"Any friend of Fran's," he said, tipping his glass my way. He took a long drink.

"What about the officer?" I asked. "Was he tailing me, too?"

"Nah." It was LaCroix. "Saw Billy coming down the street. Figured a guy wearing a uniform and a gun would be impressive."

"Certainly worked," I said. "Can't figure out why they pulled that routine. They must know I'm meeting their boss tomorrow."

"They were messing with you," LaCroix said. "They do that a lot."

"Think we're all hicks," Warren said. "Nobody likes them. Word gets around pretty fast when they're back on the island. They'll cause trouble someplace. Always be a next time."

"Why doesn't DeMio rein them in?" I said.

"Maybe he doesn't care," LaCroix said.

"Why don't you ask him, Michael?" Warren said.

"Think I will."

"Figure you're gonna piss him off anyway, talking about the Abbott murder, so why not?"

"Does everyone know I'm here to talk to DeMio?"

Warren shook her head. "It's not you," she said. "It's him. Everything DeMio does is fodder for gossip, speculation and *Godfather* fantasies." She looked at LaCroix. "What'd we talk about before the mob bought the Brewster cottage?"

"Can't remember," he said, "but it's time for me to go." LaCroix drank the last of his beer and stood up. "Michael Russo."

I looked up at him.

"Take care of yourself."

"I will. Thank you." LaCroix reached into his pocket for money. "Beer's on me," I said. "Least I can do."

"Thank you," he said. "Fran, good night."

"Night, Henri," she said. We watched him leave the bar.

"Nice man," I said.

"He is, but don't let that fool you. He's a tough guy in a fight," she said. "Toughest around here, anyway."

"Will he be following me tomorrow?"

"Be a good idea, don't you think?"

16

I woke to the sound of rain hitting the roof. I clicked my iPhone. Seven-thirty. I'd drifted off to sleep last night reading Steve Hamilton's *A Cold Day in Paradise.* As in Paradise, Michigan. My damp, chilly morning on Mackinac was still more spring-like than Paradise, on the shores of Lake Superior, an hour north and an hour colder. I put the bookmark inside the novel and set it on the table next to the bed.

I sat up and stretched my arms over my head. I had enough time for an easy run before I met DeMio. Mackinac Island is a runner's delight. Hills, trails, stairways, the eight-mile loop around the Island on the shore road. Choose a route and have at it. No better place.

I grabbed socks and a pair of navy running shorts from a side pocket in my bag. I pulled on the same long sleeve t-shirt as last night. "I'm gonna get wet," I said to no one. I laced up my Asics and zipped up a rain jacket. I took my iPad and went for coffee.

"Good morning," I said to the several people scattered around the dining room that was only steps from my first-floor room. I filled a cup with coffee from the urn on the sideboard and sat down at a small two-top table.

Before leaving the office yesterday, I downloaded a PDF of the information Hendricks emailed me about the DeMios, father and son. Reading up on Joey could wait. I flipped the cover and opened the file.

Carmine DeMio was born in 1940 in Naples. He immigrated with his parents to East Kingston, New York, two years later. Five years after that, the family moved to a row house on Chicago's Near South Side. In 1996, he moved to a condo on the Gold Coast where he still lived. Plus the East Bluff cottage on Mackinac Island.

He worked his way to the top of the Baldini crime family until his supposed retirement in 2010. His primary source of income was, or is, drugs, prostitution and loan sharking.

I closed the cover on my iPad. Knew more about DeMio and the Mafia, but that didn't help me with Abbott's death. Time to run. A few minutes later, I took Market Street to Cadotte and headed up the long hill to Four Corners. I often used running to come up with a new angle on an old problem. As it was, I still had no plan for talking with DeMio.

The rain came down steadily but without wind. I hit a comfortable pace by the time I passed the airport on my way to Crooked Tree. I wondered what DeMio'd tell me about Cherokee Point, Joey and the murder of Carleton Abbott. Maybe he knew nothing. Doubt that.

I ran by Sugar Loaf, swung around at Arch rock and headed towards the East Bluff. Thought I'd run by DeMio's house on way back. Just for fun. It was easy to spot in the middle of the row of bluff cottages. A huge, gleaming white house with a curved porch that faced south and east. Two of the porch windows were open. The other end of the house was obscured by tall oak trees. A new cedar-shake roof was a long way from the weathered gray it would become. No sign of activity. No gun turrets either.

It was still raining when I stopped running at the Cloghaun, fifty-one minutes after I began. A little over five miles. I used the private door rather than drip sweat through the lobby.

The hot shower felt good on tired muscles. I wanted to look resort-dressy, if there is such a thing, at breakfast, so I chose khaki pants and a brick red polo shirt. A sweater might have made sense in the damp air, but I wanted DeMio to know I wasn't carrying. I grabbed my jacket, a hat and went out into the rain for the walk to the Marquette Park Hotel.

17

F ive minutes later, I walked into the lobby of Carmine DeMio's hotel. I shook the wet off my jacket and hat and hung them on a coat rack near the front door.

I stopped at the archway to the dining room. It was a large, open room with a long, heavy, dark bar at the rear, near the kitchen. Tables of all sizes spread forward towards large glass windows at the front of the room. They offered a beautiful view of the park, the marina and the harbor. Nice spot for a meal alone or with friends.

"Good morning, sir," said a voice with a distinctive Jamaican accent. I turned away from the windows to see an elegantly dressed man in his fifties, about six-one, holding menus. His nameplate read, "George Reed."

"Good morning," I said. "I have an appointment . . ."

"Right this way, sir." And off he went to a corner table at the front of the room by the windows. The table would sit six easily, but only two places were set this morning. Mr. Reed went around the table and pulled out a chair. "If you please, sir," he said, "Mr. DeMio will join you shortly." He put down only one menu, in front of me. Obviously, I was expected.

"Good morning, sir," said another Jamaican, this time a woman in her twenties. She wore a black skirt, below the knee and a white, short-sleeve shirt. She put down two glasses of water. "Coffee and juice, sir?"

"Coffee, please," I said, "no juice." She looked over her shoulder and nodded. A man, short and thin and not Jamaican, appeared, poured coffee and vanished. Quickly.

I sat with my back to a sidewall, so I could see out the windows and down the expanse of the dining room. I sipped some coffee. Just as I put my cup down, I saw him at the bar. Santino Cicci. He sat on a stool, his back against the bar, facing the room. He wore black slacks and a tan shirt covered by a black cotton jacket. Bet he was packing under the jacket.

I looked around the room for Gino Rosato. Didn't see him at first, then I noticed him just outside the dining room. He'd stuffed his walrus-like body into a wingback chair and had a clear view of the table. He wore a jacket, too.

A big man, six-three, maybe, appeared at the dining room door. Probably in his seventies, the man was heavy with the soft weight of too much food and drink. His neck pressed tightly against his black shirt collar. He wore a gray sharkskin suit and a black tie. His hair was black, thin and combed straight back.

The man put his hands on his hips in a way that seemed to fill the archway. He surveyed the room with all the intensity of a general at the battlefield. Without ever having seen a picture, I knew it was Carmine DeMio.

The maître d' greeted him, menus in hand. DeMio went first, knowing precisely where he was going.

"Mr. DeMio," I said, extending my hand as I stood up, "Michael Russo. Glad to meet you."

DeMio ignored my greeting and went around the other side of the table to his chair. Then he shook my hand, firmly and sat down. The little man with the coffee appeared, quietly, poured coffee for DeMio, left a glass of orange juice and retreated. DeMio looked up, raised his hand and the little man came back to refill my cup.

"What'll you have for breakfast," DeMio said, as if we'd been chatting for a while.

Before I could answer, our waitress arrived, without a notepad. "I'll have the usual," DeMio said to her.

"And for you, sir?" she said to me.

"What is 'the usual,'" I asked DeMio, but the waitress answered.

"Eggs Benedict, sir."

"Order it," DeMio said, "best on the island."

I nodded and the waitress left.

"What do you want, Russo?" It was both a question and a demand.

"I want to talk about the murder of Carleton Abbott."

"Don't know anything about Abbott," he said, drinking some coffee. "Don't care either."

"You know the Abbotts?"

He nodded. "And the other tight-asses who run that place."

"Cherokee Point," I said.

"Yeah."

"Think Abbott was killed by one of his neighbors?"

For the first time since he sat down, DeMio looked right at me.

"Those candy asses?" he said. "Little men with guns? I hope you're smarter than to think that, Russo." He drank some orange juice. "Only thing they kill are bottles of booze."

The waitress put down two plates of Eggs Benedict without saying a word and left. The coffee man reappeared. He replaced our cups with fresh cups and poured in steaming hot coffee. Didn't ask for a new cup. Must be a standing order for DeMio.

"I don't think Abbott was killed by a neighbor either," I said. "The only serious suspect has been cleared." I cut into my eggs. Good eggs. Even better Hollandaise.

"Abbott's kid?"

"Uh-huh. Nickelson Abbott."

"What kind of name is that? Nickelson." DeMio shook his head, still chewing some eggs.

"It's an earlier generation's . . ."

"I know what it is," he said, impatiently. "What I don't get is why you'd tag your kid with somebody's last name."

"Me either," I said.

A small, pencil-thin smile appeared on his face. DeMio nodded. "Maybe you're smart, after all," he said. "Try this one. Who will the cops pick up next?"

"Who do you think?" I said.

"I know who's next," he said, "I'm askin' you."

"Your son."

DeMio finished a bite of food, wiped the napkin across his mouth and sat back. "Joseph," he said with a hint of a sigh.

"Obvious choice."

"Of course it's the obvious choice. It's always the obvious choice when we're around. Blame it on a gangster from Chicago. Gotta be him." DeMio leaned forward and towards me. "Even when it isn't."

"You sure about that?"

DeMio nodded. "He was here all night."

"At your house?"

He shook his head. "At the hotel. He lives in a small suite, on the third floor. In the back. Don't wanna spoil the kid," he said and laughed.

DeMio started for his coffee, but stopped. "Russo," he said, "why you helping the cops? What's your game?"

Do I tell him the truth? Make it up? Pretty savvy guy. "You know Don Hendricks?"

DeMio nodded.

"And Martin Fleener of the State Police?"

"Of course."

"They're decent guys with a job to do," I said. "Asked me to help with the boys at Cherokee Point. Lotta stonewalling. Thought I might do better."

"Did you?"

I shrugged. "Not much. I seemed to have antagonized the powers that be."

DeMio laughed, deeply, loudly. People at the next table looked our way, furtively.

"Good for you, Russo," DeMio said, smiling broadly. "Good for you." DeMio looked from side to side, as if he were about to share a secret and leaned forward. "My boys woudda antagonized 'em." He laughed again. Nobody looked.

"Why are you asking me questions? Why not Fleener?"

"Keep things low key," I said. "They come here, you go there. Either way gets attention. I ask the questions, maybe not." I picked up my cup and drank some coffee.

"Never known the cops to be so thoughtful."

"It's not you, it's . . ."

"It's the blue bloods at Cherokee Point," he said.

"Yep," I said.

"So whaddya want to know, detective-man?"

"Joey and the Abbotts. Cops know about the money and drugs."

DeMio shrugged.

"They know about Parker and Joey."

"The love birds," he said. "What's that have to do with anything?"

"Any connection between Joey and a member of the Abbott family spells trouble for Joey. You know that, right?"

DeMio nodded, slowly. "Told Joseph to stay away from that place. Those people are trouble." The waitress appeared, but DeMio waved her away. "Joseph makes plenty of money. Doesn't need Nick's gambling debts. Plenty of broads, too." He waved again and the waitress appeared, cleared our plates without a word and left. "But no, he says, 'lotta money to be made down there, Pop,' he says. 'The snobs are dumb,' he says. He wanted more out of the blue bloods." DeMio shook his head. "Tried to tell him."

"What about Parker Abbott?"

"Came on to Joey. At one of her brother's cocktail parties. All tits and ass. He's been humping her ever since."

"Think the cops would be interested in Joey if he wasn't involved with Nick or Parker?"

DeMio shook his head.

"Me, either," I said.

"Think he'll be picked up for routine questioning?" he said.

I nodded.

"You know this how?" he said.

"Already done. Be my guess."

"You seem to know a lotta things, Russo." DeMio's voice was edgy. "Still a civilian?"

I nodded.

"Not working for the cops?"

I shook my head.

"Might not believe you if Joseph gets charged. Remember that."

"Your threats don't worry me. Even with your goons in the room," I said, gesturing towards Santino Cicci at the bar.

"You're not alone either, pal," he said and pointed down the row of window tables.

I turned around. Three tables down sat Henri LaCroix, with a cup of coffee, reading *The New York Times*. Didn't know he was there.

"Look, Mr. DeMio," I said, "I help Hendricks, it helps you."

He waved and the little coffee man reappeared. He poured fresh coffee for DeMio. I shook my head and covered my cup.

"How's that, Russo?"

"If Joey's in the clear, it'll keep Hendricks off your back. And Joey's. Make it harder for a couple of members of Congress to pressure the cops."

"Ah, yes, Senator Randall Harrison from the good state of Indiana. That little prick's had a hard-on for me for years. Chairs a Sub-Committee on Investigations. Came after me in Chicago. Corruption, loan sharking, bribery. He refused to quit, but he never got me."

"Be nice to keep it that way."

He nodded. "It would." He looked like he'd think about it. Maybe.

"Thank you for the breakfast," I said, putting my napkin on the table. "And the conversation."

"You're welcome," he said.

"Before I go," I said, "I've got some advice for you."

"You've got advice for me?" DeMio said, surprised.

"That's right."

"You got balls, Russo, I give you that," he said shaking his head, almost smiling.

"Got nothing to do with Cherokee Point."

"I'm listening."

"Call off your goons," I said. "Tell Laurel and Hardy to quit rousting the locals."

"What they do for fun is on their own time," he said, "I don't have anything to say about that."

"Bullshit. You have everything to say about that," I said. "Call 'em off."

"Why should I care?"

"Because people hate you for it. The goons and you." DeMio listened, but that's all I could tell. "Look, you want to be part of the Mackinac community," I said.

He gave me a dismissive sneer. "I have a house here. That's all."

"No, it's not," I said. "You bought the Brewster cottage in 2010. Been here every summer since. You show up hours after the water's turned in the spring. Don't leave until the frost threatens the waterline in the fall. You even get a room for the Christmas Bazaar in December. And you donate Chicago hotel rooms for Island fundraisers. That's more than owning a house. Call 'em off."

"You're a strange guy, Russo. One minute, you're a friend to the cops, the next, you're the goddamn Chamber of Commerce."

DeMio stood and pushed his chair back. We were done.

I stood. "You were right," I said.

"About what?"

"The Eggs Benedict."

DeMio nodded, then turned on his heels and exited the dining room with the same authority and energy as he entered it. Santino Cicci got off the bar stool and followed his boss. He glanced my way for a moment.

I walked down the row of window tables and stopped at the man hidden behind a newspaper. "Nobody reads those things anymore," I said, pointing at the dead-trees version of The *Times*.

LaCroix lowered the paper and looked up at me. "I do," he said. "Like the feel of the paper, smell of the ink."

"You have coffee here often?"

He shook his head. "Not in years. Lousy coffee." LaCroix folded the newspaper and stood.

"You keeping an eye on me again?"

He ignored my question. "You headed out?" he asked.

I nodded.

"I'll walk with you."

18

I took my hat and jacket off the coatrack. The rain had turned into a thick mist. Fog hid much of the harbor's east breakwall. I zipped the jacket, pulled the collar up around my neck and put on my hat.

"You must think it's still raining." I looked over my shoulder. It was La Croix. He wore a dark green Gore-Tex shell. No hat. "Which way you going?" he asked.

"Cloghaun,to get my bag."

"I'll go that way, too," he said.

We walked down the hotel's curved driveway to the sidewalk. The mist did not deter tourists. Families, couples and singles roamed up and down the street. Dock porters with bags piled precariously high in their bike baskets, the UPS dray and three horse-drawn taxis all struggled for space on a congested Main Street.

We walked in silence for a few minutes, navigating the crowded sidewalk. We turned up the hill at Doud's. When we got to less busy Back Street, I said to LaCroix, "What do you do when you're not doing this?"

"You mean tagging along with you?"

"Uh-huh."

"A little of this and that," he said, "but mostly I'm a landlord."

"Seriously?"

"Yep. A small apartment building in the village. Four units. I also own a building on Main Street, near the Shepler's dock. Apartments up, two retail stores down. Work some construction in the winter."

"Born here?" I asked.

"Born and raised," he said. "I also went to college, Northwestern, worked in Chicago for a few years. In finance. Nice city, Chicago. Made a lot of money in a short time. Moved back to Mackinac eleven years ago. Bought a house and the buildings. Never married. Close once."

"Like the Island better than Chicago?"

"Like it different than Chicago," LaCroix said. "Those are the basics. Any more questions?" he said, slowly.

"I hear you're a pretty tough guy in a fight."

"On the Island long enough, you hear lots of rumors," he said. "Wouldn't pay much attention, if I were you."

"Fran Warren's the one who told me you were tough."

"Oh, um, well. . ." He tried to say something, but the words couldn't get out. "Fran's a good woman."

I stopped. La Croix went four more steps before he caught himself and turned around. We were in front of City Hall, at the corner of Astor Street.

"Never known Fran to make things up," I said.

La Croix shuffled his feet, looked down towards Main Street.

"Mr. La Croix . . ."

"Henri."

"Henri," I said, "I appreciate your concern for my safety. Fran's, too. But I can get to the Cloghaun and the boat dock without an escort."

"Probably so," he said. "But after last night at the Mustang, I'd be wary of DeMio's men."

I told La Croix what I told DeMio about his goons.

"Until we know he's taken your advice," La Croix said, "watch your back."

"But I can get off the Island today by myself," I said, "okay?"

La Croix grinned broadly and nodded. "Okay." He reached out his hand. "Safe travels, then, Michael."

We shook hands. "Thank you, Henri." With that, he started down Astor Street.

I went to the Cloghaun and retrieved my bag. "I enjoyed my stay," I said to the woman at the desk. She wore a lime green clip in her hair today.

"I'm delighted to hear that," she said. "Please come back."

"I will," I said. I left the B&B and went down Hoban to the boat dock. No bad guys followed me. No good guys, either.

I walked down the ramp, got on the ferry and sat near the back. The mist had stopped, but the fog was thick as we left the harbor. Thicker than it seemed standing on steps of the Marquette Park Hotel.

I didn't know any more leaving the Island than when I arrived. Maybe A.J. and Sheridan were right after all. Joey DeMio really was everyone's easy choice for killer-of-the-day. Hell, even the guy's father figured he'd be accused. I didn't buy Sheridan's theory about Parker Abbott. Still . . . I punched A.J.'s number. "Hi," I said.

"How was your breakfast?" she said.

"Tell you later. Listen, I need help sorting this out. Would you call Ellen or Frank and invite them for dinner and wine?"

"And some long-winded analysis?" A.J. said, sarcastically.

"That, too," I said. "I'll do pasta and a salad."

"Okay," she said. A.J. paused, then said, "Michael?"

"Yeah?"

"You okay?"

"I am, darling," I said. "Honest. I'm just lost with this. I'm too preoccupied. Makes no sense. I need your help. And Frank's. That's all."

"All right," she said, "I'll get back to you."

Frank Marshall was the first person I wanted to talk with. He made a living investigating things. Besides, he always wanted to be my mentor. My consigliere, as he put it. Time to give him a chance. Throw in A.J.'s nose for news and maybe the four of us could come up with a new angle. Sure needed one. That or I'm stuck with Joey DeMio. That'd make it damn near unanimous.

I got off the ferry in Mackinaw City. My iPhone chirped. The screen read, "Four 4 pasta. I'll get baguettes at Crooked Tree. Love you."

Well, that's a start. Of course, if it finished and Joey was still the chief suspect, I'd be stuck with Santino and Gino as my new best friends for a long time.

I couldn't help but look over my shoulder as I walked from the boat to the parking lot in Mackinaw City.

19

Very little fog was left in the air as I drove south on U.S. 31. Traffic thickened quickly between Alanson and Crooked Lake. Peak tourist season was three weeks away, but you'd never know it on this road. I took Division to Mitchell to avoid Bay View and parked at my apartment building.

"Hello, Fudgie. Happy to have you back," Sandy said when I entered the office.

"Such a warm greeting," I said. "Thanks a lot."

"How was your meeting with the mob?"

"One guy, Sandy. One retired guy, that's all."

"Do they let you retire from the Mafia, Michael?" she asked, handing me a stack of messages and the mail.

"Do I look like Mario Puzo?"

"Top message is Bill Stapleton. Wants you to call. Said it's about Cherokee Point."

I punched the number. "Hello, Billy," I said. "What's up in the Motor City?"

"Same old," he said.

"Buy a new Porsche yet?"

"Could be," Stapleton said. "Drove a slick Carrera S last week. Red over navy leather."

"You drive too fast for a red sports car," I said. "Cop magnet."

"Yeah, yeah."

"You'll need a good lawyer," I said.

"I am a good lawyer," Stapleton said. "And you're the one who'll need a good lawyer you keep harassing my clients at Cherokee Point."

"What's that mean?"

"Means you pissed off Wardcliff Griswold. Wants to sue your ass. Said you invaded his privacy, his words. Said you insulted and demeaned him and Nickelson Abbott. Any of that true?"

"How'd Griswold find out we knew each other?"

"Figure you told him," he said.

"Nope," I said.

I told Stapleton about my visit to Griswold's cottage.

"So you didn't accuse them of being mobbed up?"

"Of course not," I said. "Bet Joey DeMio checked me out and found the connection between us."

"Could be, I suppose."

"Did Griswold ever mention the dead guy?" I said.

"Don't think he cares much about Carleton Abbott."

"Me either," I said.

"Cool it with those folks, will you," he said. "I don't want explaining why we can't sue you to become a habit."

We talked cars for a few more minutes, then said good-bye. I couldn't shake the notion that we were stuck on "privacy" and "image" and "secrecy" at Cherokee Point.

I made a few calls to clients and one prospect who was interested in buying an old Victorian three-story not far from A.J.'s house on Bay Street. Most of the mail went into the wastebasket.

"I'll head home in a while," I said to Sandy. "Frank Marshall and Ellen Paxton are coming for dinner."

"What are you making?"

"Pasta," I said. "Maybe Frank can help. . ."

"Olive oil and garlic sauce or Marinara?"

"Olive oil," I said. "This case is more important than dinner."

"If you say so," she said.

"Listen, if I end up at the bottom of the Bay wearing cement overshoes, you'll be sorry you wanted to talk pasta."

"If you say so, Michael," she said, "if you say so."

"You are impossible," I said. "I'm goin' home."

20

"**W**hat are you doing, A.J.?"

"Watching you, darling."

"I'm taking a shower," I said.

"I can see that."

"Why are you watching me take a shower? Frank and Ellen'll be here pretty soon."

"I was just thinking," she said.

"What?" I said. "I can't hear you."

"I wondered what would happen if I unbuttoned my shirt," she said, loud enough.

"We'd be late for dinner?" I answered, hesitantly. A.J. wore black Capri's, black Chaco sandals and a wide-striped red and white shirt, which she unbuttoned, one button at a time, starting at the top. She smiled. When all the buttons were undone, A.J. slipped the shirt off her shoulders and it dropped to the white tile floor. No camisole, no bra.

"That's what I thought would happen," she said. A.J. turned and walked towards the bathroom door. She stopped, turned again and walked back. "Almost forgot this," she said, bending down, ever so slowly, to pick up her shirt. "We're having company for dinner, dear." A.J. flung the shirt over one shoulder and went back towards the bathroom door.

"Hey," I said, almost shouting. "Anyone ever tell you that you're a tease?"

I toweled off, brushed my hair and put on khaki shorts and a brick red long sleeve t-shirt. It read, "Nantucket" on the front.

The dining room table was set for the four, with bowls for pasta and salad, bright red cloth napkins and two large, red candles. When I got to the kitchen, A.J. was tearing red-leaf lettuce into bite-size pieces.

She'd already cut up green onions, part of a cucumber and some cherry tomatoes. "Will you make the dressing?" she said. "The one with the Fustini's Balsamic?"

"Sure," I said. "But only after a kiss." I pulled her to me, wrapped my arms around her waist and kissed her.

She looked up at me. "Nice," she said.

I nodded. "Felt good."

The chime sounded. "I'll get it." A.J. went to the door and buzzed the outside lock to let Marshall and Paxton in.

"Hello, you two," A.J. said. I dried my hands and joined them at the front door.

"Here, I brought this," Ellen said, handing me a bottle of Chardonnay. "Figured you'd make pasta, but I know you prefer white wine."

"Yes, we do," I said. "Sit down. I'll open the wine. Got some horseradish cheese, some Parmesan-Reggiano, too."

Marshall and Paxton sat on the living room couch. A.J. put the cheese board on the coffee table and took one of the side chairs.

I uncorked the wine, grabbed four glasses and joined them in the living room.

"Thanks for coming on such short notice," I said.

"Happy to be here," Frank said, "and I don't have to cook tonight."

"Reminds me of the old days," Ellen said. "Talking about cases."

"You?" A.J. said, surprised. "He was the investigator," she said, pointing at Frank.

"Sure, sure," Ellen said. "Frank used me as a sounding board all the time. Doesn't Michael talk to you about his cases?"

"Uh-huh," A.J. said.

"It was seldom gossip," Ellen said. "Hardly ever idle chitchat. It was usually serious."

"Smart enough to know I couldn't think of all the angles," Frank said. "That's where Ellen came in."

I poured wine into four glasses.

"A toast," I said. "To a couple of smart guys who always need help."

"Smart enough to eat some cheese," Frank said. He cut a chunk of horseradish cheese and took a cracker. "Smart enough to do that."

I slid the wine bottle into the chiller on the table. We cut pieces of cheese, took crackers and put them on small plates.

"Okay, I'm ready," Ellen said.

"Why don't you update us, Michael," Frank said. "Start after you pissed off Wardcliff Griswold. We know that story."

"Does everybody know about that?"

"Small towns," Ellen said.

"And powerful people who tell other powerful people when someone, in this case you," Frank said, pointing at me, "offends them. Offends their sense of propriety, invades their privacy."

"Funny that whenever Cherokee Point is mentioned, the talk eventually gets to invading someone's privacy."

"Not funny to the folks at Cherokee Point," Frank said.

"Guess not. Okay," I said, cutting more cheese, "I'll update you, then get dinner ready while the three of you decide what I oughta do." I sipped some Chardonnay. "I expect a full report over pasta and a salad. Agreed?"

"Agreed," they all said, raising their glasses in a show of comic solidarity.

"You guys are a big help." I gave them a recap of the story, then went into the kitchen.

I put on water for the penne and turned up the heat. I poured olive oil into a large frying pan and added more than a pinch of red pepper flakes. I chopped up fresh garlic and threw it in the pan. When the water boiled, I added the pasta and turned up the heat on the frying pan.

I used some of the chopped garlic to make the salad dressing A.J. wanted.

"A.J.," I said from the kitchen. "You want to toss the salad?"

"No," she said.

Well, okay then. I drained the pasta, put it in the olive oil sauce and tossed it to coat the penne inside and out. I dumped the mixture into a large white serving bowl, threw on several pieces of fresh basil and took it and the salad bowl to the table.

Frank, Ellen and A.J. were at the table, waiting, barely able to keep from laughing as I put the serving bowls down. Each of them held a knife in one fist, a fork in the other. "Some crime fighters you are," I said.

We served ourselves and were eating when Frank said, "Were you surprised that Nick Abbott had an alibi?"

I nodded. "Especially one that checked out so easily."

"Which made Joey DeMio," A.J. said, "the heir apparent killer for just about everybody."

"You gotta admit," Frank said, "he's got motive, opportunity and means." Frank ate some salad. "With Carleton Abbott dead, Nick inherits lots of money. Right?"

I nodded.

"Enough money to pay off the gambling debts, buy more drugs and keep Joey a happy man."

"Does that mean you think DeMio's the killer?" A.J. said. "Not just an easy pick because he's a gangster?"

"That or he ordered the murder," Frank said.

"I'm sure Hendricks and Fleener find it easy enough to believe," Ellen said.

"What about Kelsey Sheridan?" Frank asked. He looked at me. "He told me his theory of the case, too."

"Parker Abbott?"

Frank nodded.

"For crissake, Frank, he wants to be a mystery writer."

"Sharp guy," Frank said.

"Maybe so, but he likes to invent things."

"Funny how Sheridan's theory keeps popping up." It was A.J.. "Must be my reporter's nose," she said, "but I smell a rat someplace. This thing just doesn't gel."

"You think Sheridan's right about Parker?"

My iPhone buzzed noisily on the sideboard next to the table.

"Let it go," A.J. said.

"Too many people got my number," I said, "Senators, congressmen. Who's next?" I got up to get the phone.

"Could be the Mafia calling?" Frank said, and laughed.

"It's 312 area code," I said when I picked up the phone.

"That's Chicago," Frank said.

"It is the Mafia," A.J. said, and they all laughed.

"Shut up! All of you."

I swiped the pad. "Michael Russo."

"Good evening, counselor," the voice said. "This is Joey DeMio."

"Good evening, Joey DeMio," I said, looking at my dinner companions. I thought Frank would drop his wine glass on the floor. "How'd you get this number?"

DeMio ignored my question. "I think it's time we had a little chat, counselor," he said.

"I'm listening."

"You in your office tomorrow morning?"

"I can be," I said.

"I'll be there at ten," DeMio said, and the phone went dead.

I put the iPhone back on the sideboard. I looked over at the table.

"Well," I said. "Anybody got a smartass remark?" I stood with my hands on my hips. "Anybody?"

"No," Ellen said, shaking her head.

"Me, either," Frank said.

"Oh, sit down," A.J. said, "and eat your damn dinner."

"That really Joey DeMio?" Ellen said.

"Yes," I said.

"I think I'm gonna need more wine, Michael," Ellen said, lifting her empty glass off the table.

I went to the kitchen, got another bottle of Chardonnay from the refrigerator and opened it.

"What'd he want?" A.J. said when I got back to the table.

"He's coming to the office tomorrow morning." I poured wine. "Wants to talk."

"About what?" Frank said.

"Didn't say."

"Doubt he wants to confess," Frank said. "Might want to tell you his side of the story."

"We'll see," I said. I sipped the wine. "So where were we?"

"I wanted more wine," Ellen said.

"I need more salad." It was A.J.

"Got any bread left?" That was Frank.

I shook my head. "You guys are worthless crime fighters, but a helluva lot a fun."

"Here-here," A.J. said, and raised her glass.

"Here-here," Frank and Ellen said.

Frank stood up. "I'll help clear the table." He picked up his plate and a serving bowl. "One thing concerns me, Michael."

"And that is?"

"A gangster everyone pegs as the killer of Carleton Abbott will be in your office tomorrow."

I nodded.

"Be careful, will you, Michael," Frank said. "Please."

21

I rolled over and looked at the clock. It was seven.

"You running this morning?" A.J. asked, moving her body over against mine. She lifted her arm and put it across my chest.

"Uh-huh," I said. "A short one."

"Maybe we should take the day off. Stay here all day."

"Sooner or later, you'd get too hungry."

"Only hungry for you, darling," she said.

"Oh, please."

A.J. lifted her head off the pillow. "It's seven in the morning. You expect witty repartee?"

"I'd settle for coffee."

We tossed the covers back. A.J. put on a white terry cloth robe and went to the kitchen. I grabbed a pair of red running shorts from the dresser next to the bed and put on a black t-shirt.

By the time I got to the kitchen, the coffee was ready. I poured a mug full and sat at the small, white wrought-iron café table by the window. A.J. came in barefoot, dressed in jeans and a gray sweatshirt. She poured coffee.

I picked up my phone, found Sandy Jefferies' number and punched it.

"Morning, Michael," Sandy said.

"Hope I didn't wake you," I said.

"Getting my daily dose of *Morning Joe*," she said, "and coffee."

"Who's Scarborough ranting about today?"

"Been on Mika's case for the last few minutes."

"Nothing new there," I said.

"Nope, but you didn't call to chat about Mika and Joe," she said.

"Joey DeMio's coming in at ten," I said.

"You want me to get out the red carpet?"

"Probably won't come alone. Keep an eye out for his goons. In case they show up first."

"Want me to get Danish? Make them coffee?"

"I want to make sure you don't throw them out of the office."

"Ah, I won't hurt 'em," Sandy said. "Can I go now? Bill de Blasio's on."

I said good-bye and put down the phone.

"More coffee?" A.J. said.

I nodded and she refilled my mug.

"Are you as concerned about this morning as Frank was last night?"

"Not really," I said. "What's DeMio gonna do? He's not likely to pull anything in the office. If he wanted to hurt me, it wouldn't be there."

"I hope you're right," A.J. said.

I strapped on my running watch. "Gotta go, babe. It's getting late."

"I'll be gone by the time you get back."

"You in the office all day?"

"Uh-huh. New edition goes up overnight. Lots of last minute stuff."

I got up, put my mug in the sink and kissed A.J. "Call you later."

"Okay."

I left the apartment and stretched outside for a change. It was warm already. Humidity was up, too. Shouldn't take long to get my legs loose. The water in the bay glistened with streaks of sunlight. The maple trees along the street seemed greener, somehow, against the bright blue sky. I need to remember mornings like this when I'm trying to run in February, in single-digit temperatures and a twenty-mile an hour wind off the ice in the Bay.

I clicked my watch and started up Rose Street. By the time I got to Bay View, I moved smoothly, almost effortlessly, and could focus on Joey DeMio's impending visit.

Only two alternatives seemed reasonable. Like everyone else in Northern Michigan, DeMio knew I was working the Abbott case. He might be curious about what I knew. I'd tell him. Not much. Wonder if he'd believe me? He'd assume the cops were interested in him. He might figure I knew just how interested. Of course, he might want to tell me his whereabouts on the night of Abbott's murder. Not holding my breath on that one, and he probably talked with Carmine.

I held a steady pace, a little over eight minutes a mile. Bay View was getting busier every day. Painters, landscapers, building people. Summer people were returning to open their cottages. It wouldn't be long before the streets of Bay View were just as congested as downtown Petoskey.

The other alternative for DeMio's trip to my office was simpler. He did not like my involvement in the case and wanted me to quit snooping around. How might that one play out? He tells me to stop. I say no. He threatens me. I say, screw you. Stalemate. Unless he brings his shooters. Then we got a different ballgame.

I pulled up, clicked my watch off. I was breathing steadily and sweating hard. The sun was higher now. The streaks of light across the bay were gone, but the water was a deeper, richer shade of blue.

Hard to tell which alternative seemed more likely. If DeMio has backup with him, well, then I'll know.

22

The shower felt particularly good. A good run in summer humidity is hard. I made a small pot of coffee and dropped an English muffin in the toaster.

I picked out a pair of lightweight gray slacks, a blue button-down shirt and a navy and red striped tie. I'd add a navy blazer to look professional. Might even impress Joey DeMio.

I sat at the kitchen table, ate the English muffin with raspberry preserves and went through my email. Nothing needed my immediate attention. It was nine-thirty. I put the dishes in the sink, grabbed the blazer and left for the office.

My eyes darted up the street and down. I watched the side street and tried to look at every car coming at me. Did I need to be this vigilant? Rather than take the usual shortcut through the parking lot behind Lake Street, I continued up Howard, then turned on Lake. DeMio's guys wouldn't waste time in a parking lot. They'd be on the street. There was nothing. Nothing that I saw anyway.

I opened the office door. Gino Rosato leaned against the sidewall of Sandy's office, his arms crossed over his chubby chest. His dark brown suit was rumpled and too small at the same time. Sandy was not at her desk. Rosato lifted himself off the wall and took four slow steps across the room, passing the doorway to my office. He leaned against the opposite wall and crossed his arms.

"Mr. Russo," said a deep, clear voice. A figure appeared in the doorway. "Won't you come in?" The man was five-ten, about 185 and 50 years old. He stood erect, with the alertness of a man who worked out regularly. He wore a dark gray, three-button suit over a white shirt with a deep purple tie. His eyes were round, his skin medium-dark. The hair was black, not long, and combed straight back. Just like his father.

"Joseph Carmine DeMio," the man said and reached out his hand. "A pleasure to meet you."

I hesitated.

"It's all right, counselor, she's right here," he said, pointing to his right. "Ms. Jeffries?"

"I'm fine, Michael," Sandy said from inside my office.

I shook DeMio's hand. It was just firm enough. He wasn't trying to prove anything. He stood aside and I walked past him. Sandy sat in one of the captain's chairs at the side of the room, near the window. Against the other wall was Santino Cicci. He didn't lean on the wall. He stood, almost at attention, feet slightly apart, arms at his side. His suit jacket was unbuttoned. He waited to see what I would do.

"Have a seat, Mr. Russo," DeMio said. "In your chair, please." I didn't remember gangsters being this polite in the movies. Unless they were about to shoot you.

I walked around the desk and sat in my chair. DeMio sat in the other captain's chair, opposite my desk. Rosato came into the office and leaned against the inside wall. He did not close the door.

I looked over at Sandy. She looked back, but didn't say anything.

"It's all right, Mr. Russo, Ms. Jeffries didn't expect three of us this morning."

"I guess not," I said. I looked first at Cicci, then at Rosato. "Do you need Laurel and Hardy to keep an appointment with me?"

DeMio raised his hands, put one palm on each side of his head and slowly smoothed his hair back. He brought his hands down. "I'll let that one go, counselor," he said, "in the interest of goodwill. But don't push your luck."

"So," I said, "why did you want to see me?"

"Thought we might straighten a few things out," DeMio said. "I know that you've been helping the police with their investigation of the Abbott murder." He crossed his legs and smoothed out the crease in his pant leg. "What have you learned so far?"

Hmm. Maybe I was wrong about why Laurel and Hardy are here. Maybe the guy's just curious.

"I know the cops are looking at me for this. A guy gets himself dead, the cops want to talk to me." He shook his head. "Never fails."

"The cops already talked to you," I said.

"What does that tell you?" DeMio said.

"Nothing. Except they didn't arrest you."

"They did not," he said.

"They don't have enough to hold you."

"They do not." He leaned back in the chair. "What can you add? Based on your investigation."

"Nothing," I said.

"Nothing? What do you mean, nothing?"

"Abbott's dead. Nick's got an alibi. You're a suspect. That's it."

"The cops figured that out by themselves. What do they want you for?"

"My pleasant personality? My winning smile?"

Sandy put her head down, her left hand rubbed her forehead. Either she was stuffing a laugh or cringing. Not sure which.

DeMio sat erect in the chair. He didn't look happy. "All right, Russo," he said, "here's how it's gonna go." Apparently, he was done being polite. Then he stood up in front of the desk. "I don't trust you. I don't trust your motives. Right now the cops got nothing. I got more to worry about if you're snooping around. No more helping the cops. No more asking questions. Understand? Go file a divorce or something."

"Don't have any divorce cases," I said.

Sandy's forehead was still getting a rub down.

"Okay, smart guy, let me make it clear." DeMio put his hands on the desk, palms down, and leaned forward. "Do what I tell you. Or my friends here will use more persuasive ways of getting your attention."

"Is that a threat?"

"Yes."

I shrugged.

"Stay on this case, you get hurt."

"Gentlemen," a voice said. I looked up. In the doorway stood Henri LaCroix. "Not a move, gentlemen. Unless I say so." LaCroix closed the door behind him. "Mr. DeMio, turn around, please, slowly."

DeMio did as he was told.

"Thank you."

We all looked at LaCroix.

"Mr. Cicci, there's no reason for you to move. Keep your arms at your side. You, too, Mr. Rosato."

Cicci wasn't ready to concede the moment. He made a slight move to his jacket.

"Stop. Not going to tell you again." With that, LaCroix raised his right arm at the elbow. He held a "Gen 4" Glock. With a Lex silencer. We all saw it.

"Mr. Russo, would you relieve Messrs. Cicci and Rosato of their weapons? Mr. Cicci first."

I walked to Cicci and pulled back his jacket. Nothing. I carefully reached behind him, under his coat. A small .38 sat in a holster in the middle of his back. I slipped it out of the holster. I went behind my desk, put down the gun and moved to Rosato. His gun, also a .38, was in a holster on his right hip. I put it on my desk, too.

"Thank you for your cooperation, gentlemen. We'll assume that Mr. DeMio has no weapon."

DeMio put one hand on each side of his suit jacket and slowly pulled it open. Nothing. He let go of the jacket and dropped his hands.

"Listen carefully, gentlemen." LaCroix said, "No one bothers either Michael Russo or Sandra Jeffries. Not on the street, not in a car, not at home. You got that?" LaCroix reached for the door handle and turned it to open the door. "Now walk out of the office slowly and keep going. Do not come back."

DeMio went first. When he got to the door, LaCroix put out his hand and stopped him. Cicci and Rosato stopped, too.

"One more thing, DeMio," LaCroix said. "Watch your back. You never knew I was here."

The three men left the office. I heard them go down the stairs.

I looked at LaCroix. He smiled.

"You got a license for that?" I said, pointing at the gun.

"License for what?" he said, grinning. He put the gun into a shoulder holster under his tan poplin jacket.

"Never mind," I said. "Want some coffee?"

LaCroix nodded.

"I'll get it," Sandy said. "Gotta do something to get the blood moving again." She stopped and looked at me. "'Don't have any divorce cases?' They got guns. You got a smart-mouth. Are you out of your fucking mind?"

"I thought it was funny," LaCroix said.

Jeffries looked at LaCroix and shook her head. "You're as bad as he is," she said. "Whoever you are."

La Croix smiled and reached out his hand. "Henri LaCroix, Mackinac Island. Pleased to meet you."

Sandy shook his hand. "Men," she said, and went to get coffee.

23

LaCroix sat in a captain's chair. I was behind the desk.

"You out there long?"

"Long enough. Didn't want to intrude." He arranged himself in the chair and leaned back. "When Joey D. threatened you, well, I decided to intrude."

"Glad you did," Sandy said, coming in with three mugs of coffee. She put them on the desk and sat down in the other chair. I reached for a mug. So did LaCroix. He took a swallow of coffee.

"Ah, that tastes good. Thank you," he said to Sandy.

She nodded. "Least I could do since my boss, here," she pointed at me, "was about to get us killed."

"It wasn't that bad," I said.

"It was that bad. They had guns. What did you have?"

I shrugged and drank some coffee. It did taste good.

"One question," Sandy said, looking at LaCroix, "how did you get here?"

"Car. From the St. Ignace ferry dock."

Sandy rolled her eyes. "I'm gonna look for another job."

"Sorry," he said. "Actually, I've been in town for a couple of days. Your boss has a way of annoying people. Not good if those people have guns."

"See," Sandy said, "what'd I just say?" She shook her head. "People with guns scare me."

"Guns should scare you," LaCroix said. "But DeMio's men won't start anything serious without an order from Joey. Or Carmine."

"You really think this is serious?" I said.

He nodded. "Serious enough or DeMio would have arrived with his lawyer instead of those two guys."

I leaned forward and put my elbows on the desk. "You gonna hang around until the Abbott thing is done?"

"Well," LaCroix said thoughtfully, "I got some shopping to do. Home Depot. Symons General Store. Stuff like that."

"Another smart mouth," Sandy said. "What is it with you two? Somebody else has to get dead before you take this seriously?"

I didn't say anything. Neither did LaCroix.

Sandy looked at LaCroix. "What are you, anyway? A bodyguard? A private eye?"

"A landlord, actually," LaCroix said.

"A landlord?"

"Yep. Have lease, will travel."

Sandy stood and picked up her coffee mug. "I've got work to do," she said. "When you two frat boys want to play it straight, let me know." She went out and closed the door behind her.

"We really that bad?" LaCroix said.

"Sharp woman. Doesn't miss much," I said. "Pretty quiet work most of the time. An angry husband once in a while, but we've never had much gun trouble."

"Better not to have it now, either," LaCroix said.

"Which begs the question. You planning to hang around?"

LaCroix nodded. "For a while, anyway. Got plenty of time right now. Besides, I like Petoskey. I like the Perry Hotel. The restaurants."

"Okay," I said, "Fran Warren asked you to go into the Mustang the other night. You show up at the hotel. Now this. Fran ask you to come down here, too?"

LaCroix picked up his mug, but it was empty. "Michael, we've watched Carmine and Joey for three years. Their goons, too. Pretty mean bunch. They can cause a lot of trouble real fast. But, yeah, Fran asked me to keep an eye on you until this was finished."

"You're backing up a guy you don't know just because a friend asked you to. That right?"

"That and Fran Warren's my sister. Big sister, actually. Always do what she tells me. Thinks you're a nice landlord. Good building, low rent, honest guy."

I started to laugh.

"Besides," he said, "I've had a couple of run-ins with Cicci and Rosato. They hassle the locals, I hassle back. Keeps 'em honest."

"You consider me a local?"

"Probably not, but I get a chance to fuck with Joey D. on this one." LaCroix smiled.

"So where do we go from here?" I said.

"Don't know about you, but I'm headed for Home Depot."

"That's not what I meant."

"I know what you meant," LaCroix said. "Look, live your life. I'll be around. This'll be over in a few days anyway. Cops'll arrest DeMio pretty soon. That ought to do it, don't you think?"

"If he killed Abbott," I said.

"You don't think he did?" LaCroix said, a bit surprised.

"Everybody seems to think so."

LaCroix looked at his empty mug again. "Time to go," he said. He got out of his chair and reached across the desk. I stood and we shook hands.

"Thanks," I said.

LaCroix nodded, turned and went out of my office.

"Have a pleasant day, Ms. Jeffries," he said.

24

I looked up. Sandy Jeffries leaned on the doorjamb.

"What?"

She didn't move. "More coffee?" she said.

I nodded.

Sandy picked up my mug. She came back, put two mugs of fresh coffee on the desk and sat down.

I picked up the mug and drank some coffee. "Okay. Something's on your mind," I said. "Besides your critique of my behavior."

"Michael, you do good work in this community. You help people. You earn a living."

"You, too," I said. "You're part of it, too."

"I know," Sandy said, "but today." She shook her head. "This was playing in a different league."

"Because of the guns?"

"Yes, because of the guns," she said. "And the people who had the guns." She drank some coffee and settled back in the chair. "The cops come to you for help. You annoy the snobs at Cherokee Point. Different stuff for us. Kinda interesting, to be honest. But today . . ."

"We've had a client or two wave a gun. This is rural Michigan, after all."

"It's not the same, Michael," Sandy said. "These guys are pros. . . They treat guns the way farmers treat plows."

"Sandy, nothing happened. A lot of hot air. LaCroix's right. Nobody'll start trouble unless DeMio, father or son, orders it."

"Listen to yourself, Michael. Do you hear yourself?" I raised my hands from the desk, palms up.

"You're rationalizing gun play," she said.

"There was no gun play, Sandy. LaCroix saw to that."

"Because our gunslinger outfoxed their gunslingers? Is that you're saying?"

"Well, he did."

"And who is Henri LaCroix, anyway? A landlord? A guy with a gun and a silencer? You buy that bullshit?"

"What he said."

"Must be some pretty nasty renters on Mackinac Island.

"Must be."

"Ah, Michael," Sandy said. "How did we get from Cherokee Point to this?"

I got up and pulled down the window sash behind me. Heavy clouds had rolled in. The wind had picked up off the Bay and cooled the air. Rain wasn't far off.

"Sounds like you've given this some thought, Sandy. What's your take?"

"Well, Hendricks asking you to go to Cherokee Point was one thing. Pretty innocent. Doing a favor. It got more exciting when Joey DeMio's name got tossed into the mix. All that changed when he became a suspect."

"Yeah."

"Hendricks should have pulled you out right then," Sandy said.

"He gave me the chance."

"Hendricks?" I nodded. "You said no?" I nodded again.

"Michael. Are you. . ?"

"I was already in it, Sandy. Told Hendricks I'd help. Didn't want to quit on him."

"You're doing it again. This isn't *High Noon*, and you're not Gary Cooper. Listen to yourself."

"Being overly dramatic, don't you think?" I said.

"Am I?"

25

I poured two glasses of Sauvignon Blanc and took them to the front porch. A.J. sat on a white wicker loveseat with her feet on a small coffee table. Like the rest of her house, the porch had been restored with a new floor and new spindles for the railing. Bay Street was quiet. Most of the neighbors were home from work already and few tourists ever ventured this far from the Gaslight District. Away from the windy Bay, the late afternoon air was still warm. The clouds still promised rain.

I went back to the kitchen. I tore a Three o'clock baguette into five big chunks, put them in a basket and picked up the cheese board. I put the bread and cheese on the coffee table next to a large candle and joined A.J. on the love seat.

We sipped wine, talked some, were quiet some. We held hands when it didn't get in the way of nibbling cheese and bread. I told her about my morning and Sandy's unflattering assessment of me. "That's about it for my wacky day," I said, "how's life at the paper?"

"Not as exciting as yours, that's for sure." A.J. cut a piece of horseradish cheese left over from dinner and tore a chunk of baguette. She took a bite. I knew what she was thinking.

"Here's the thing," she said. "My work is exciting, too. Because it's challenging, unpredictable and intellectually stimulating. We don't know if the new version of *PPD Wired* will work or not." She picked up her glass and took a small sip. "But the Abbott case. I don't know, Michael." She shook her head. "Your morning was exciting, but it's not a healthy excitement. It's destructive excitement. And it's dangerous."

I turned towards her and put my hand on her arm. "It's not that bad," I said. "Those guys weren't going to start anything in my office. Besides, Henri LaCroix was there."

"I'm glad he was there," she said sharply, "but that's not the point."

"What is the point?" I said. I didn't like where this was going.

"Murder. Gangsters. Guns. You don't think any of that is crazy or bad. That's the point."

"Come on, A.J., you sound like Sandy. This'll all be over in a few days."

"Maybe there's a reason I sound like Sandy," she said. "You just don't listen sometimes. Or don't want to listen."

"I always listen to you, sweetheart."

"Don't patronize me, Michael."

I put down my glass and turned towards her. "Sorry, A.J.," I said. "I don't mean to be glib or to patronize you."

She leaned over and kissed me lightly on the lips.

"It's just . . . it's something else," I said.

"I know," she said. "I can tell."

"You can?"

She nodded.

"It's the way you've talked about the Abbott case from the start. You're animated. It's exciting for you. Gangsters and guns make it more exciting. The danger's fun, isn't it?"

"Yeah," I said. I tore off a chunk of bread. "Didn't want to admit it, but there it is." I bit into the bread and took a piece of Parmesan-Reggiano.

"Want some more wine?" she said.

"Uh-huh."

A.J. got up and went inside. The house was quiet and peaceful. Bay Street was quiet and peaceful. Life was quiet and peaceful. Not a bad thing. Yet. . .

A.J. came back from the kitchen and filled our glasses. She put the bottle on the floor, next to the love seat and sat down.

"You remember the Clarkston divorce?" I said. "Left her husband in the Sault. Moved down here."

"That the husband with the crazy brother?"

I nodded.

"Threatened to kill you a few times?"

"That's the guy."

"What happened to them?" she asked.

"Granting a divorce was easy for the court when hubby and his brother kept waving guns around to make her come home."

"Why are you bringing up that old case? Three years ago? Four?"

"Think it was 2011," I said. "You remember Hendricks cut the red tape and got me a carry permit?"

"I remember."

"Same feeling back then," I said. "Something about it."

"Three mobsters with guns is a lot more to worry about than the Clarkston brothers," A.J. said.

"I'm not so sure. Clarkston was fueled by emotion, by rage. He could go off like a rocket. Not DeMio. Everything he does is calculated."

"That's reassuring," A.J. said.

I looked at A.J. "It's getting late. Want me to start dinner?"

"What're we having?"

"Sandwiches. Got shaved turkey, some Provolone, croissants. Fresh tomatoes. Chips, too."

"Okay," she said, "I'll wait right here with my feet up. Call me when it's ready."

I went to the refrigerator. I arranged on an oval platter the shaved turkey, slices of Provolone and two croissants cut lengthwise. I sliced the tomatoes, tore some leaf lettuce and put them on the platter. I got out dill pickle spears, mayonnaise and emptied a small bag of kettle chips into a bowl. I put it all on the table in the kitchen, with napkins, silverware and two glasses of ice water.

I walked to the front porch. A.J. sat holding her wine glass in both hands, feet still up. "Dinner's ready."

She looked up at me. "Be right there."

I went back to the kitchen. A.J. came in carrying the wine glasses and the wine. She poured more wine and sat down. We assembled the sandwiches. I bit off a large chunk. Good, but it'd be better when the summer gets rolling and Bill's Farm Market had local tomatoes.

"Tasty fixings, darling," A.J. said.

"Thanks," I said and leaned over and kissed her on the cheek.

"Tomatoes'll be better in a few weeks."

"Yep."

"You don't suppose," she said "that your need for excitement is a mid-life crisis, do you?"

I shook my head while I chewed. "I'm too young for a mid-life crisis," I said. "Besides, I already got a sports car. And how much weight could this skinny runner lose?"

"And," A.J. said, raising an index finger in the air for emphasis, "you already got a hot babe wildly in love with that skinny body."

"You can say that again."

"You already got a hot babe . . ."

"Cut that out, for Pete's sake," I said, laughing. A.J. raised her wine glass in mock toast. I raised mine.

"I have to admit," I said, "I think I could be good at this. I always liked it when I had to investigate my own cases. Didn't happen that often, but I always did a good job."

"Hoodlums with guns are dangerous, Michael."

"I'm not minimizing the danger, A.J., but I dealt with Carmine DeMio pretty well. Didn't trust him, but I respected him. Talked with him straight up. No bullshit. He recognized that. Or else why'd he listen to what I had to say?"

"Let me see if I understand," A.J. said, with just a touch of sarcasm. "You figure out how to communicate with a Mafia boss, but you piss off the president of Cherokee Point, the son of the dead guy and a United States senator, all in one meeting, no less. And you think you're good at this investigatin' thing?"

"Rookie mistakes," I said, feeling a little defensive. "I'll get better." I took the last bite of my sandwich. "I'll get better," I said, still chewing.

"Make it quick," A.J. said. "The next time Joey drops by, let's hope Henri's not busy being a landlord."

"That's not funny."

"Not trying to be funny," she said. A.J. ate two chips. "What about Joey?"

"Joey was playing a role. Carmine's retired, so to speak. Joey's in charge, more or less. He runs Cicci and Rosato. Wants to act like it."

I picked up our plates and put them in the sink. "He might threaten again, but most of it's bluster." I picked up the platter and water glasses. I turned on the faucet to rinse the dishes for the dishwasher. "I doubt that Joey, or Carmine for that matter, will do more than that unless . . ."

"Unless, what?"

I turned the tap off. "Unless Joey DeMio is charged in the death of Carleton Abbott."

"Could that happen?"

"Yeah," I said. "Just questions right now, but, yes, it could happen."

A.J. poured the last of the wine into the glasses and took them to the living room. I cleared the rest of the table, put the dishes in the dishwasher and joined her on the couch.

"Darling," A.J. said, "where's your gun?"

I looked at her, but the question did not sound strange or out of place. It might have a month ago, but not now. "In the bottom left drawer of my desk, next to the tape dispenser. Leather holster's there, too."

"Cleaned and oiled?"

"Yes."

"Carry permit up to date?"

"Yes."

"Ammunition?"

"In the drawer."

"Any practice shooting lately?"

I shrugged. "Couple of months ago, I think. Maybe longer. Every so often, I go up to the Sportmen's Gun Club. The one just south of Alanson. You know it?"

A.J. shook her head. "You a member?"

"Fifty bucks. Every year. Like clockwork."

"Perhaps a little practice is in order."

26

I opened one eye, then the other. I heard rain, hard rain hitting the window. A.J. was already out of bed. The bedroom door opened, slowly and A.J. peeked in.

"Good morning, darling," she said, as she came in the room. "Hope I didn't wake you."

"Early meeting?"

"Uh-huh." The thunder banged over the bay. "That was a loud one," she said. A.J. slipped off her white terry robe and hung it on the inside of the closet door. She wore dark green polka dot bikini panties and a matching bra. "I know what you're thinking, dear," she said.

"Not thinking," I said, "just ogling."

"You're very sweet. You really are, but an ogle is all you get this morning. I can't be late."

"Okay," I said, trying to feign disappointment.

"Coffee's ready. Sit with me while I eat a muffin."

"Okay." I got out of bed, grabbed my robe—a bigger version of A.J.'s, and stopped in the bathroom.

A.J. was at the kitchen counter. She wore a charcoal two-piece suit with a man-tailored jacket cut just below the waist and a straight skirt hemmed above the knee. A white blouse was under the jacket. Very professional. Very appealing.

I took a mug from the cupboard, poured some coffee and sat down at the table. A.J. handed me two napkins. I sipped some coffee. Tasted good.

Her muffin popped, Lucy Ricardo style, out of the toaster. She caught one of the halves in mid-air.

"Nice catch."

"One of these days," she said, "both halves."

A.J. sat down, spread a little butter on a muffin half and took a bite. "Michael, while I was in the shower, I was thinking about last night."

"You weren't wishing my body was in the shower with you?"

"Of course I was," she said, "but I need to be serious. Gotta leave in a few minutes."

"Okay."

"Well, last night got me thinking. I really meant what I said about the practice range."

"I know that," I said.

"If this is what you want to do, you know, investigate things, it wouldn't hurt to stay sharp with a gun." A.J. shook her head. "I can't believe I just said that." She bit off a piece of muffin and got up to pour more coffee.

"I get the idea," I said.

"Look, Michael," she said, "what I'm trying to say, and not very well, is that I'm with you. If this is what you want to do, I support you." She sat back down. "But it's not just the gun. You need to take care of yourself. You've got to be more alert. Be more aware of your surroundings, especially if you're on a dangerous case." She sipped some coffee.

"I can do that," I said. "Realistically, most things that need looking into won't be dangerous at all. It wasn't the Abbott killing that got you rattled, it was Joey DeMio."

She looked at her watch. "Oops, I gotta go."

"Leave the dishes," I said. "I'll take care of them." She nodded and got up.

"You running this morning?"

"No. Too much rain. Lightning, too."

A.J. grabbed her coat and briefcase and went for the door. She looked back at me. "I love you, you know."

"I know."

27

I kept the basics at A.J.'s house: khakis, sweaters, shirts. One dressy outfit, a black blazer and charcoal slacks. And running gear. I put on an old rain suit and wrapped my brief bag in a kitchen-size plastic bag. I tugged a Tigers baseball hat down tight. I went out the door and headed for home.

The rain had let up some, but lightning and thunder still broke the stillness of the morning. Maybe I could run after work. I walked straight down Bay Street and turned at Howard. The wind pushed the rain harder the closer I got to the Bay.

I closed my apartment door and left my bag in the plastic sack on the floor. I hung the wet gear on the hall tree.

I made some coffee, got out a box of corn flakes and went for a shower. A.J. accepted the change to my career path. That felt good because it was something I liked doing. Her concern for my safety was reassuring, too.

I put on a fresh pair of khakis, pleated, a light blue button down shirt and a dark green crew neck sweater. A.J.'s not the only one who can wear green.

I checked my email at the kitchen table while I ate the corn flakes, with milk, and drank coffee.

The rain turned into a steady mist on the walk to work. The sky was growing lighter in the west. I might get that run in later, after all.

"Good morning, Michael," Sandy said. "Mail's not here yet."

"Any messages?"

"One. Don Hendricks. Wants you to call him."

"Say what it was about?"

Sandy shook her head. "Think he wants to see you."

"Call him back, would you," I said. "Schedule an appointment. Whenever is okay with me." I unwrapped my brief bag and hung my coat on the rack, near the door. "Have I got anything today?"

"Robin Savage," Sandy said. "Everything's ready for her divorce hearing. She'll be here at three."

I walked into my office. Sandy followed.

"You want coffee?"

I shook my head. "Thanks. Had enough." I sat behind the desk. "Sit down for a minute."

She sat in the captain's chair in front of the desk. "What's up boss?"

"Had a long talk with A.J.," I said. "About some of the things we went over yesterday."

"You mean Joey DeMio, guns and Clint Eastwood-like landlords?"

"Yeah. That sort of thing." I told Sandy the gist of last night's conversation.

"Behind every man is a strong . . ."

"That's enough, smart-ass," I said. "She was trying her best."

"Me, too, Michael. If A.J. is behind you, so am I. But I still have reservations about the whole thing. Just so you know."

"I understand that," I said.

Sandy got up. "This case doesn't add up, Michael. When it finally does add up, I don't want it to be a threat to you."

"I understand that, too."

"I'll call Hendricks. The Savage file's on your desk."

"Thanks," I said. I opened the divorce file. Thirty-eight-year-old Robin Savage wanted a divorce, her husband wasn't contesting it. Apparently, Mr. Savage wanted to spend more time with his twenty-something girlfriend. Mrs. Savage is happy to have him gone. Pretty tame stuff compared to dealing with retired gangsters and the Laurel and Hardy boys.

Sandy came to my door. "Hendricks expects you in an hour. His office."

28

Don Hendricks leaned back in his chair. His tie was loose, his jacket hung on the back of the door. He didn't look happy. After he told me about his sit-down with Joey DeMio, I had a good idea why.

"So you're not getting anywhere?" I said.

"I wouldn't say that, but if we're gonna arrest a guy with expensive lawyers, I want it right."

A knock on the door. "Come in," Hendricks said. Martin Fleener walked in and shut the door behind him.

"Gentlemen," Fleener said, "good morning." Impeccably dressed, as always, Captain Fleener wore a black two-piece suit over a white shirt with a maroon and black striped tie. He carried a Burberry raincoat over his arm.

"Have a seat, Marty," Hendricks said. "I filled Russo in on our talk with DeMio."

"Tell him about his alibi?"

"Not yet. Waiting for you."

"Me? How thoughtful," Fleener said sarcastically.

"You guys are a lot of fun," I said. "What alibi?"

Hendricks gestured at Fleener. "Go ahead," he said, "your case."

"Said he was with Parker Abbott."

"Uh-huh."

"All night," Fleener said.

"All night?" I said.

Fleener nodded.

"Where?"

"Motel. Over by the casino." Fleener pointed in the general direction of M-72.

"It check out?"

"Man fitting DeMio's description signed in as Joseph Jones of Indian River. Paid cash."

"Joseph Jones?" I said.

Fleener nodded.

"Parker Abbott with him?"

"Nope," Fleener said, "at least no one saw her."

"What does Parker have to say?"

"Well, that's where things get interesting." It was Hendricks.

"I'm shocked," I said. "Shocked there's gambling in the back room."

"Uh-huh," Hendricks said, "me, too."

"What'd she say?"

"Spent the night with DeMio."

"So what's the problem?"

"That's all she said." It was Fleener. "DeMio was quite specific. What time they got to the motel, how many times they did it, what time they got up in the morning, that sort of thing."

"Let me guess," I said. "Parker offered no specifics."

Fleener shook his head. "She might have told us more if her brother wasn't in the room. Don't know."

"You let her brother sit in the interrogation room?"

"Talked to her at the house," Fleener said. "At Cherokee Point."

"Better if it were here," Hendricks said. "But that wasn't gonna happen."

"Did she have a lawyer?"

Fleener shook his head. "Just her brother."

"Didn't this whole thing start because the boys at Cherokee Point were throwing their weight around?"

Fleener and Hendricks nodded at the same time. I looked at Hendricks first, then Fleener. "Pressure?"

"Senator Harrison's office started the ball rolling," Hendricks said. "Lot of calls. 'You can't embarrass poor Parker by hauling her in for questioning.' That sort of thing."

I shook my head. "Okay, what now, Don?"

Hendricks put his hands behind his head and leaned back in the chair. "Right now, DeMio is a better alibi for Parker Abbott than she is for him. But she's not the suspect, he is." Somewhere in the back of my brain, Kelsey Sheridan's theory popped up.

"Ever think Parker's lying?" I said.

"Of course," Fleener said. "First thing I thought of. Question is why? Why would she tank DeMio's alibi?"

Kelsey Sheridan's theory of the case bounced around in my head again. Parker would need Joey to take the fall if she'd killed her father.

"Got a couple more leads to check out. Not sure how promising," Fleener said. "We'll talk to Parker again, but if all we end up with is her sketchy alibi," Fleener shook his head, "it'll get tough for Joey real fast."

"We bring DeMio in again," Hendricks said, "we charge him with murder."

"You'll tell me if you do that, right?"

"Yes," Hendricks said.

"Before it happens?" I said.

"I can do that," Hendricks said.

"Like Carmine to hear the bad news from me."

"You getting chummy with the mob, Michael?" Fleener said. "Your new best friend?"

I rolled my eyes at the thought and the three of us laughed. But I wondered why I wanted Carmine to hear it from me, that his son would be charged with murder.

29

"**W**ell, gentlemen, think I'll head back to the office." I got out of my chair.

"One more thing, Russo," Hendricks said. "Before you go." He pointed at the chair. I sat down.

"We heard about your little, I dunno, what should we call it, Marty, a little chat?"

"Sure. A little chat will do."

"Your little chat with Joey DeMio."

"He stopped by the office. So?"

"We know that," Hendricks said.

I looked at Fleener. "You following DeMio?"

He smiled. "Let's say we pay attention when DeMio or his men come to town."

"You object to me talking with DeMio?"

"Not at all," Hendricks said.

"Then what's this little song-and-dance all about?"

"How did you get Henri LaCroix in this?"

"LaCroix?" I said. "Is that what this is about? Henri LaCroix?"

"He a friend of yours, Russo?" Hendricks said.

I shook my head.

"Just happened to stop by your office when DeMio was there?"

"As a matter of fact, yes," I said.

Hendricks and Fleener said nothing.

"You following LaCroix?" I said to Fleener.

He shook his head.

I thought for a minute. "LaCroix following DeMio?"

Fleener shrugged. "Could be," he said, "could be."

"The question is why LaCroix would follow DeMio," Hendricks said.

"Look, you guys, I'm not playing cute here. I really don't get where this is going."

"Where'd you meet LaCroix?" Hendricks said.

"Mackinac Island. At the Mustang. A few days ago."

"He just appeared out of nowhere and you bought him a beer? A guy you didn't know."

"Come on you guys," I said. "I never saw LaCroix until he came into the Mustang. I was getting jammed by DeMio's goons. Cicci and Rosato. You know 'em, I assume."

"We do," Hendricks said.

"LaCroix got them to stop rousting me. End of story."

"And in your office?" Hendricks said.

"He walked in when DeMio was there. Simple as that." I still couldn't figure out why they were so interested in Henri LaCroix.

"Another rousting?" Hendricks said.

"In a manner of speaking. DeMio threatened me. Warned me off the Abbott case. Thinks I'm causing him more trouble than you are."

"And LaCroix convinced him otherwise?"

I shook my head. "Just told him to leave Sandy Jeffries and me alone. He was quite convincing at that."

"I'll bet he was," Hendricks said. "What do you know about Henri LaCroix?"

"Not much," I said, "but I have the feeling that you're gonna tell me."

Hendricks nodded slowly. He reached over and pulled a thick manila folder out of a side drawer. He dropped it on the desk and opened the cover.

"Henri Pierre LaCroix. Born on Mackinac Island, well, in St. Ignace, actually, 1970. One sibling, Frances Warren, of Petoskey and Mackinac." Hendricks looked up from the file. "You know Ms. Warren, I believe."

I nodded.

"She's his half-sister, to be accurate. Same mother, different fathers. LaCroix grew up on the Island, school, jobs, that sort of thing. Graduated from Northwestern University with a degree in finance. Magna Cum Laude. Smart guy. Worked for a couple of banks for a while."

"I know most of that," I said. "And he made a lot of money in Chicago, then bought property on the Island."

"It's what came in between that makes the guy interesting," Hendricks said. "He enlisted in the Army."

"Lots of people do that," I said.

"But not a lot get to Fort Benning."

"Ranger school?"

"Uh-huh. One tour in Afghanistan, then back to Benning as part of the Ranger Training Brigade. The RTB, that's what they call it, runs the school." Hendricks looked up again. "One tough guy."

Explains LaCroix's cool handling of DeMio and Laurel and Hardy.

"Left Benning in 2003 and hired on with Blackwater USA. You heard of that outfit?"

I nodded. "Mercenaries. Started by a Michigan man, I think."

"Yep. LaCroix worked as an instructor at Blackwater's private battleground in North Carolina. LaCroix left Blackwater in 2004, after the killings in Fallujah. Went back to banking in Chicago. Eventually Mackinac." Hendricks closed the cover on the file.

"Unusual bio, but what's your interest in LaCroix?"

"LaCroix's trouble. Doesn't usually create it, but when he shows up, trouble shows up, too. Mackinac County keeps an eye on him. We help 'em out down here."

Hendricks leaned back. "The question is still how did you get LaCroix in this?"

I didn't see any reason not to tell them.

"LaCroix keeps an eye on Cicci and Rosato. Nobody on the Island likes them. They cause people a lot of problems. LaCroix does his best to stop that."

"He does that job better than you think. That's why two counties are interested in the guy."

"When I got tangled up with DeMio, got hassled by Cicci and Rosato, Fran Warren asked him to help even the odds. Gotta admit, I don't mind having him around."

"Okay," Hendricks said, "just so you know who you're dealing with."

"Seems pretty soft-spoken and easy-going to me."

"Don't let that fool you, Michael," Fleener said. "LaCroix's tough enough, he doesn't have to go around proving it."

"I'll keep that in mind. Now, if there's nothing else," I said and lifted myself out of the chair.

Hendricks shook his head. "You got more, Marty?"

"Nope."

"Then I'm on my way." I opened the door, stopped and looked back at Hendricks. "You'll let me know before you charge DeMio?"

"Said I would."

30

I put my jacket on as I left the building. The rain had stopped and the clouds were breaking up. I walked down Lake Street feeling hungry and a little confused. Food would be easy to get between here and the office.

I pulled out my iPhone and punched the office number. Sandy answered.

"On my way back," I said. "You up for a little food and some conversation?"

"You bet. Where are you now?" she said.

"At the park, across from City Park Grill."

"Stop at the American Spoon Café. I want a Panzanella salad."

"Okay," I said. "Back in a few minutes."

I went in the Café. An attractive woman in her twenties with shoulder length auburn hair and soft round eyes smiled as I approached the counter. College students were starting to show up for their summer jobs. Oh, to be in college again.

"Good afternoon, sir," she said.

Sir? Guess I'm not in college. "Hello," I said, looking at the big menu. "This is to-go. One Panzanella salad and one chicken breast sandwich."

"Would you like bean salad or potato salad with the sandwich?"

"Potato salad, please."

"Be ready shortly," she said.

I paid the tab, dropped a tip in the jar and sat by a window to wait. Pennsylvania Park had turned summer green. Lawn mowers moved steadily across the grass at the Mitchell Street end of the park. Summer meant tourists breaking the easy pace of winter and spring, but part of the excitement of living downtown was the energy that came with them each summer. It wasn't so much a breath of fresh air as it was a welcome shot of adrenalin.

I wasn't sure what I should do about Henri LaCroix. At the moment, I didn't want to do a thing. The guy helped me out of a couple of jams. He seemed to be a pretty interesting guy and Hendricks information only made him more so.

"Your order's ready, sir," the woman said.

Sir, again. Oh, well. I picked up the bag, smiled a thank you and left the Café.

I stopped for the light at Howard. Two cars moved slowly through the intersection in the middle of the Gaslight District. Before too long it would be several cars. In each direction. Summer was almost here.

31

"Hi, Michael," Sandy said when I got to the office. I put down the lunch bag and hung up my jacket.

"I've got water in the refrigerator and I made fresh coffee."

"Water now, coffee later. Thanks. I'll clear some room on my desk to eat."

We sat down and unwrapped the food. Sandy handed me a bottle of water. She had water and coffee for herself.

I unwrapped my chicken sandwich and took a bite of potato salad. I was hungrier than I thought. I opened the bottle and drank some water.

Sandy took a fork and dug in. "Terrific salad," she said. "Love the fresh mozzarella."

We talked and ate. Mostly we ate.

"Blackwater, huh."

"Yep."

"Bunch of cowboys with a capital 'C', if you ask me."

"No argument there. They got a new name these days," I said.

"Whatever." Sandy drank some water and followed it with a sip of coffee. "Does answer some questions, however."

"Such as?"

"Such as how easily LaCroix handled our Mafia friends. Two of whom, I want to remind you, were armed. Like he'd done it all before."

"Probably has," I said. "Good enough to be an instructor."

"That, too. Also explains how he got in here so quietly that none of us heard him."

"A point not missed by Mr. DeMio, I'm sure."

Sandy nodded. "Didn't stay at Blackwater very long." She stuck a cherry tomato and popped it into her mouth. "Wonder why?"

"Maybe I'll ask him. The guns, the army, even working for Blackwater may not be the whole story."

"Could be he's not the gunslinger he appears to be," she said.

"Unless he needs to be."

"You want more coffee?" I said, getting out of my chair.

Sandy shook her head.

"Be right back." I grabbed a mug. It said "Interlochen Center for the Arts" on the side.

"Where do we go from here?" Sandy said.

"Not sure. Until Fleener arrests Joey, I guess we wait."

Sandy looked puzzled.

"Something else?"

"Two things," Sandy said. "You thought about talking to Parker Abbott?"

"Several times," I said. "Keep putting it off."

"Why?"

"Well. . ." I hesitated. "I guess I'm not sure what to ask. You know, like which questions will help, which won't."

"Be less lawyer and more investigator. Perry Mason always wants to know the answer before he asks the question. Sam Spade just starts digging." Sandy put her mug on the desk. "Start digging."

"What's the other thing?"

"You ignoring my Perry Mason analogy?"

"You got a more relevant literary lawyer for your analogy than Perry Mason?"

"No," Sandy said. "It's my analogy. You're ignoring me."

"No, I'm not," I said. "I'll think about it. What else?"

"Kelsey Sheridan," she said.

"What about him?"

"Every time there's a new wrinkle in this case, you bring up Kelsey Sheridan or his pet theory. Maybe you ought to talk with him again in light of all you've learned in the meantime."

"Can't talk about many of the details with him. Wouldn't be appropriate."

"You don't have too," Sandy said. "Just tell him you'd like to hear it again. His case for Parker as the killer."

"He's a smart guy. He'll wonder why I'm asking."

"Let him wonder," she said. "He'll understand why you can't talk about it. Invite him back to the office."

"Maybe I should."

"I'd have Frank Marshall there, too," Sandy said. "He's been at this a lot longer than you have. Might pick up something you miss."

"He just might," I said. "Call both of them. Marshall first, and set it up."

"Will do," Sandy said.

We heard a knock at the outside door. Sandy got up to answer it as the door opened. I could not see the doorway from my chair.

"Hello," Sandy said, "Can I help your, sir?"

"You certainly can, young lady." The voice was vaguely familiar. So was the tone.

"My name is Wardcliff Griswold. I'm President of Cherokee Point Resort Association."

"Well, I'll be . . ."

Gotta get out there before Sandy tosses a sarcastic hand grenade. I came through the doorway with a big smile. "Ward," I said, greeting him like a long lost tennis buddy. "How's things at the Point? Getting ready for the cocktail party season, are we?"

Griswold hesitated, not a frequent occurrence, I'm sure. "Ah, yes, hello, Mr. Russo. So nice to see you." He reached out to shake my hand.

"Call me Michael, please," I said, taking his hand. "What can I do for you?"

"I realize I'm without appointment, but if I might have a few moments of your time, I'd greatly appreciate it."

"I'm free right now. Won't you come in?"

I stepped aside and waved Griswold into my office with a grand sweep of my arm. He walked by me. I looked back at Sandy. She stuck her tongue out. With gusto.

pointed to the empty chair in front of the desk. Griswold sat down. He wore a navy blazer, double-breasted, over a light blue shirt, no tie. His gray, worsted wool slacks had a perfect crease. His black penny loafers were polished within an inch of their lives.

"What can I do for you, Ward?"

He seemed uneasy. "Do you think we might have some privacy?" he said, pointing over his shoulder towards my office door.

"I'll close the door if you like, but everything said here is held in strictest confidence." Not true, of course. Griswold wasn't a client, but Sandy'd let me have it if she didn't hear this first hand.

"Well, all right then," he said and settled into his chair. "I need to discuss something most urgent."

Maybe I'm too cynical in my middle years, but I couldn't wait to hear what Griswold considered "most urgent."

"As you know, I am president of Cherokee Point."

I nodded.

"As such, I'm responsible for the well-being of our residents." Nervously, he reached to straighten the knot of a tie that wasn't there. "Many of them are quite upset with people poking around all the time."

"Poking around?"

"Yes," he said. "You know, people from town."

"Like the police or the coroner's office," I said.

"Exactly," Griswold said. "Snooping around. Asking questions. You see what I'm saying, don't you?"

"Just doing their job, Ward," I said.

"Yes, well, they ought to do it somewhere else, don't you think?"

This conversation had a familiar feel. It probably wasn't going to end well. But let's be optimistic, shall we?

"You do see what I mean?"

Guess I didn't answer fast enough. Griswold had an expectant look on his face.

"Ward," I said, not knowing where I was going. "Did something happen? I mean, like, recently?"

"Yes, something happened," he said, emphatically. "The police interrogated Parker Abbott." He leaned forward. "Those men from town came to the Abbott cottage," he said, pointing his finger, down, at my desk, "and interrogated her."

"This is still an open investigation, Ward."

"It should be open and shut. That Chicago man, he's the one."

"Joey DeMio," I said.

"Yes," Griswold said, "him." He was nervous, edgy. "Why Parker lied for him, I don't understand. Her lawyer should have been there. Maybe if her lawyer was there, she would have kept her mouth shut, but Nickelson said he could handle it. I would have handled it diffcrently, but Nickelson didn't want me in the room. I could listen but not talk."

"You listened?"

"I was upstairs, in the sitting room, listening on the intercom. Heard every word." He shook his head. "You have no idea how embarrassing this is for the Point."

Ward was right about that. I don't have any idea. "Ward, I'll say it again, this is a murder investigation. A man from the Cherokee Point, a friend of yours, was shot to death."

"Let them have their investigation," he said, "but let them have it elsewhere." That tone, again, authoritarian and bratty.

"Might just get your wish," I said.

"What?" he said. Griswold looked as if I'd slapped his face. "What are you talking about?"

"The police will ask Parker Abbott to come in for more questions."

"More questions?"

"Yes," I said. "If she won't come voluntarily, they'll bring her in."

"When?"

"Don't know," I said. "It'll be soon, and this time, it's all business."

"Can't you do something about it?" he said.

"Me?"

"Yes, you," he said, with an edge to his voice. "That's why I came here today. I want you to put an end to this."

"I can't do that, Ward," I said. "I won't interfere with a police investigation."

"Isn't that what you did when you came to see Nickelson and me? Interfere with a police investigation?"

"No, Ward," I said. "I want to be quite clear. Don Hendricks, the county prosecutor, asked me to talk with you. He asked me . . ."

"So you'll help him, but you won't help us? We don't know what Parker might say if they get tough with her. She could expose us and you won't help us? Is that it?"

"No, Ward, that's not it," I said, raising my voice. "Hendricks asked me to talk with you because I was not from the police, not from town, as you put it. He has a job to do and the people at Cherokee Point were less than cooperative."

"I should say so," he said.

"Hendricks thought you folks might be more comfortable talking with me."

"I certainly don't understand why the man thought that."

"All right, Mr. Griswold," I said, putting emphasis on the "Mr." I stood up and came around the desk. "I have another appointment in a few minutes . . ."

"I'm sure you do," he said.

"And this conversation is getting us nowhere."

Griswold smoothed a crease in his gray slacks, stood up and buttoned his navy blazer. "Good day, sir," he said and turned to leave. "Good day, young lady," Griswold said to Sandy as he passed through the outer office. The door slammed behind him.

"Ta-ta, old chap," Sandy said.

I leaned on the doorjamb. Sandy looked at me. "Don't start," I said.

"Went about as well as the last time you talked to him," she said. "Out at good ole Cherokee Point."

"Don't remind me."

I walked to the front window and looked out. Most of the clouds were gone. The sun took over. On Lake Street, foot traffic had picked up. Seasonal businesses are about to kick it into high gear.

"You're right. That was just like last time." I shook my head.

"Yep," Sandy said.

"As soon as it doesn't go Griswold's way, the whole thing comes unglued."

"He sounds like a very old spoiled brat."

"Uh-huh," I said. "Turned into a nice day. Think I'll go run. Might clear my head."

"Can't do that," Sandy said.

I looked over my shoulder. "Why not?"

"Robin Savage will be here pretty soon. Might want to brush up on her divorce file."

33

"**R**obin Savage is here to see you," Sandy said from the doorway. "Robin, come on in."

"Good afternoon, Michael," she said and we shook hands. At five-ten, she looked like a former athlete who'd aged gracefully, which is exactly what she was. Four years as the star center of the University of Wisconsin's basketball team. She wore a burgundy linen two-piece suit with a light gray silk blouse. Her auburn hair fell to the shoulders. I met Robin Savage in 2004 when she and Carol Trent, from Boyne City, opened their own business as CPAs over on East Mitchell, a block from my office. They were soliciting new clients and I signed on. They took care of taxes and payroll for businesses, mostly in Emmet County. Sandy and A.J. are among their individual tax clients. When Robin's husband of twenty-one years decided that he preferred the company of a younger woman, "the kid with the big boobs," Robin called her, she came to me to arrange the divorce.

"Can I get you anything?" Sandy said.

"No, thanks, Sandy. Just finished lunch."

"How've you been," I said. "Sorry I missed your last call."

"Not a problem," she said. "Sandy's kept me up to date. But I am glad this is almost over."

"It'll be done next week," I said.

"You know, Michael, after the initial shock that Steven was screwing around, I thought I was okay." Robin shook her head. "It hurt more that she was younger, well, thirty-five isn't that much younger than me. I spent too much time blaming myself," she said. "I'd look in the mirror and see no shape, no figure anymore. Me. The athlete." She shook her head, again.

"You've pulled yourself out of it pretty well," I said. "You're as happy as you've been in weeks."

She nodded. "Took me a while to realize what I had. Good friends, like you, who were very supportive. Carol and I have a successful business, so I can always earn a living. And I love this city. Even walks in the neighborhood are therapy." Robin lived in a remodeled two-story on Summit Street, a stone's throw from A.J.'s. She got the house in the divorce when her husband took the cottage on Lake Charlevoix.

"So you think it'll go smoothly?" she said.

"Yes," I said. "The details are spelled out. It helps that you and Steven aren't fighting about anything."

"Only because Steven wants more time to get laid by the kid with big boobs." Robin shifted uneasily in her chair. "Sorry," she said, "didn't mean to be pissy."

"You're entitled," I said. "Trying to stuff the anger won't help."

"So you've said before."

"Besides Steven's preoccupation with his girlfriend made it easier for you to get a good settlement," I said.

"You're the one who got the settlement."

"Sure, I'm just saying."

Robin nodded. "I know," she said. "Do we need to get together before the hearing?"

"Not necessary," I said. "I'll meet you at the courthouse next Thursday at nine." I thought we were done, but Robin stayed in the chair. She looked past my shoulder, as if trying to see out the window.

"Robin?"

"Sorry, Michael," she said. "Mind if I shift gears for a minute?"

"Go ahead," I said.

"It's personal. Nothing about the divorce."

"That's okay."

"The murder case you're working on," she said, "Carleton Abbott?"

Well, that seals it. Is there anyone left in Emmet County who thinks I'm still a lawyer? "What about it?" I said.

"Have you met Parker Abbott?"

"Not yet," I said. "Why?"

"If you run into her, be careful, that's all."

I didn't say anything because I didn't know what to say.

"Our paths have crossed several times," Robin said. "I've watched her in action. Social events mostly, some charity benefits. Places where women, men and alcohol mingle." She shook her head. "She's not what she seems to be."

"What does that mean?"

"For one thing, she's a flirt, big time."

"I'm not opposed to a little good-natured flirting," I said.

"Me, either, but Parker is a predator. There's no good-natured anything to her."

I waited. Her face told me more was coming.

"It's a woman thing, Michael. We don't trust her, especially around men, our men."

"Did she make a play for Steven?"

Robin shook her head. "No, unfortunately," she said, laughing. "He'd deserve her." She hesitated for a minute. "Watch yourself around her." Robin looked at her watch. "It's time to go. You're busy and I've got work to do." She got out of the chair and I came around the desk. We walked to the door together. "Bye, Sandy," Robin said.

"Good luck next week," Sandy said.

Robin smiled. "I'm well represented, don't you think?" Robin said, gesturing at me.

"I do, indeed."

Robin Savage left the office and I went to Sandy's desk. "Did you hear any of that?"

She shook her head. "Not really," she said. "Had work to do. Couldn't have been half as much fun as good ole Wardcliff."

"Smart-ass."

"Thank you," Sandy said, softly, as if I just commented on her clothes. "What'd I miss?"

"Robin warned me about Parker Abbott."

"Are they friends?"

"More like acquaintances. Said women don't like her."

"She's got that right," Sandy said.

I was surprised. "You didn't tell me you knew her."

"Don't. Not even acquaintances, but I've seen her. And women talk."

"What do they say?"

"Robin's right. Women don't trust her."

"With their men?"

"She's a man junkie," Sandy said. "Gotta get male attention, even if it means playing for a good friend's man. Shitty behavior, any way you look at it." Sandy leaned back in her chair. "She really doesn't have women friends, Michael."

"That bad?"

Sandy nodded.

"All right," I said. "Guess I'll put her on my radar screen." I looked at my watch. "Meeting A.J. later. Got time for a run if I get a move on."

"One more thing," Sandy said, "before you go. Kelsey Sheridan's on board to meet with you and Frank Marshall."

"What about Frank?"

"Haven't heard back," she said. "Go on, get outta here."

left the office and went down Lake Street to McLean & Eakin to pick up my copy of *The Times*. I left by the back entrance and crossed the parking lot. Over the Bay, a few puffy clouds remained from the morning's rain. I pulled out my phone and clicked twice. Sixty-eight degrees. Not bad for this time of year, or for an afternoon run.

I dropped my brief bag on the floor when I walked in the door and exchanged my street clothes for a pair of dark green running shorts and a poly T that said "Lilac Festival 10K, 2011" on the front. I laced up a new pair of Brooks Addiction. Gotta get a lighter shoe one of these days.

I set my watch at zero and took my usual route up Rose, then over to Arlington on the way to Bay View. My pace was off, not smooth. I was thinking more about Ward Griswold than my running form. Not a good idea while I was still rehabbing a strained hamstring. I was tired of Griswold. Tired of his attitude. Okay, he was a snob, but that didn't give him license to live without regard for the outside world. But that's what he did, at least when it suited him.

I turned left on Lakeview, then straight ahead on Park. Another week and the only time for a relaxed run in Bay View Association would be sunup. Too much summer traffic mixed with too many construction trucks in the afternoon.

My pace finally smoothed out. My breathing was light and steady. My body took over when my head was too busy.

Maybe Griswold's motives were exactly what they seemed. Protect Cherokee Point. Everything else be damned. He said as much every time he opened his mouth about the Abbotts or the police. And for some reason, he worried that Parker might blab to the cops about something and make things even worse. Maybe I oughta listen.

I eased into a walk as I got back to my building. A run, even a bad one, helped clarify things. I had two choices. Try to get Griswold to understand the outside world wasn't going away any time soon. Or ignore him and find Carleton Abbott's killer.

I went inside. The hot shower beat down on my head. It felt good, soothing after a difficult run. Ignoring Griswold was the best choice. Find Abbott's killer and be done with it. Done with Griswold, the Abbotts, the DeMios, the whole pack of them. Just find the murderer. I sounded more like an investigator every day.

I picked out a fresh pair of khakis, pleated, from the closet and a red and white striped polo shirt. I slipped on my deck shoes, grabbed a navy crewneck and went to meet A.J.

The early evening air was still pleasantly warm. I went over to Bay Street and across Pennsylvania Park. Maybe I ought to stop at McLean & Eakin on the way home. Pick up a couple of private eye novels. Chandler, Parker, Hamilton. Got a lot to learn.

35

The hostess, not someone I recognized, asked if I wanted a table.

"No, thank you," I said and pointed at the bar. The City Park Grill was quiet tonight. A couple of four-tops in the back and one by the front window. Two women at the near end of the bar looked my way as I walked by. I smiled. Neither had come from work, judging by their clothes. The brunette wore a tight black skirt, very short, and a tighter black top. The redhead wore a short gray skirt and white halter-top over lots of tan skin. Bet they thought my polo and crewneck were cutting edge fashion.

I sat down at the other end of the bar. "Hey, Mr. Russo," Meg Samuels said, drying her hands on a white towel. "How ya doing tonight?"

"Good, Meg. Been back to Houghton-Hancock lately?"

"The UP? No," she said, shaking her head. "Really liking Petoskey." She smiled. "Thanks for asking. Is Ms. Lester joining you?"

"In a few minutes. I'll have a house Chardonnay while I wait."

"Be right back," she said and went down the bar.

Two women, both beautiful and dressed for an evening out, came through the door and hailed the two women at the bar. Lots of "oohs" and "ahs" and big hugs. Guess they knew each other. I didn't have much else to do, so watching them have fun was pleasant entertainment.

"Careful, there, Mr. Russo," Meg said as she put a coaster and a glass of wine in front of me.

I sipped some Chardonnay. "That obvious?"

"I've seen worse," she said, laughing. "They are good lookin', I'll say that for 'em."

So they were. Practicing my newly acquired investigative powers, I deduced that one of the new arrivals was in her thirties, about five-four with short black hair. She was pencil thin, probably worked out, and wore heels that had to be four inches. Wanted to be taller, I guess. I worried she might fall over. Frontwards.

One of women called Meg Samuels. They huddled together with Meg as if plotting a dangerous caper. Meg came out of the huddle and said, "Be back in a minute." Guess they only ordered drinks. Meg picked up a wine glass and a long-stemmed glass for a Martini. She stopped near me. As she poured wine, she said, softly, "They wanted to know if you were Michael Russo." Meg put the wine bottle back on ice. She gave me a side-ways glance and said, "Careful." I nodded. Meg put the pieces of the Martini together, poured it into the tall glass, dropped in two olives and took the drinks down the bar.

My iPhone chirped. I pulled it from my pocket. It was A.J. "be a little late. wait." I tapped back, "okay."

I sipped my wine and thought about a snack. A "little late" sometimes turned into "quite a while" when A.J. was at work. I ordered a small plate of cheese and crackers. The women at the other end of the bar were still huddled. Must be planning a crime, after all.

The chatter and occasional laughter died down. One of the women emerged from the group and came towards me. She walked with a purpose. She was tall, about five-seven, maybe one twenty-five. Her blond hair was parted on the left and fell to her shoulders. It moved as she walked. She wore a black silk blouse, sleeveless, buttoned into deep cleavage, over a charcoal skirt, above the knee. A single string of pearls hung around her neck. Very striking.

"Michael Russo," she said. It wasn't a question.

"Yes."

"Parker Abbott," she said, reaching out.

"Nice to meet you, Ms. Abbott," I said, shaking her hand.

"May I sit down?"

"Please," I said, gesturing at the barstool. She put herself on the stool and nodded in Meg's direction.

"Call me Parker," she said.

"I will."

Meg brought her wine from the other end of the bar. "Thanks, Meg," she said.

"Come here often?"

"Often enough." She took a drink of wine. Not a sip.

"I'm happy to meet you," I said, "but I'm curious why you left your friends. You seemed to be enjoying yourselves."

"We are, but this is our second stop." Parker picked up her glass. "We'll meet later someplace else." She drank more wine and said, "Meg," and pointed to her empty glass. "I didn't want to pass up a chance to meet the man who caused so much trouble out at Cherokee Point." She smiled.

Meg put a small plate of sliced cheeses and crackers on the bar.

"Thanks, Meg," I said. "Be my guest," I said pointing at the plate. Parker nodded.

"You don't seem too upset about that," I said.

"Upset?" she said, laughing. "Upset? Why the hell didn't you show up sooner. Thirty years sooner."

"I was a teenager with acne thirty years ago, Parker."

"You might have been a teenager, Michael," she said, "but they don't allow acne in Birmingham, do they?" She put one knee over the other and leaned towards me. I tried not to notice the deep V in her blouse.

She drank more wine. I picked up a piece of cheese, Swiss, and popped it in my mouth.

"You seem to have me at a disadvantage," I said.

"Because I know about you?" She smiled and sat back up. "Don't flatter yourself. They had a report on you before you ever set foot in Griswold's cottage."

"They?"

"The good old boys. The Fraternity, I call 'em. You know who I mean. Griswold, Sheridan, Senator Harrison." Her eyes narrowed and she said, "And let us not overlook my father and my brother." She drank more wine. "Dormitory sophomores. All of 'em. But better alcohol."

"So I don't forget," I said, "I'm sorry for your loss."

"Thanks," Parker said, curtly. "My brother took over where he left off. Didn't skip a beat. Trust me."

"I'm not sure I understand."

"Bullshit," she said, "you understand perfectly well." She finished her wine and raised her hand for Meg. She leaned forward again and looked at me, hard. A fresh glass of wine landed on the bar. Parker nodded a thank you to Meg but never took her eyes off me. "I'll bet you found out what kind of hornet's nest you were getting into before you ever met Griswold or my brother."

I shrugged.

"Uh-huh," she said and sat back. "But their sources of information are better." She wagged her finger in mock admonishment, "unless you got a wise guy helping you, too."

"Joey DeMio?"

"Of course, Joey DeMio," she said. "Who the hell did you think I meant, Al Capone?" The "did you" came out as a slurred one word.

"I thought your brother didn't like you hanging out with DeMio."

"Like?" she said, sharply. "My brother doesn't like or dislike. He approves or disapproves. He disapproves of everything I do. He's just like Father only meaner. Didn't you do your homework?"

I shrugged. "Why'd Nick go to Joey for information?"

"Because my brother uses people. He doesn't like Joey DeMio, he doesn't trust Joey DeMio, he especially doesn't like me fucking Joey DeMio, but he needed Joey to find out about you. Better than our dimwitted lawyers." She picked up a cracker and took a bite. "No offense."

I smiled. "None taken."

"Problem was," she said, "the report didn't prepare them for you. You know, Michael," she smiled and wagged her finger again, "you were rude and nasty to them."

"Rude? Nasty?"

She leaned forward again. On purpose. "You were not deferential, Russo. One is not supposed to diss the good ole boys."

I shook my head. "I don't know whether to laugh or cry."

She sat up. "Crying would be more deferential," she said, laughing. "Just kidding."

I sipped my wine and, this time, I signaled Meg for a refill. "What did you mean when you called them dormitory sophomores?"

"This ain't rocket science. Haven't you heard the stories?"

I shook my head.

"All right," she said, "try this. The good ole boys are just that, boys. But they got money. A lot of money. Cherokee Point is their clubby tree house. They decide who gets in, who counts. And nobody counts but them and a few people who look like them."

Meg filled my glass. Just in time. I took a sip.

"They sit around, drinking expensive booze, and snicker at everyone who isn't them. Who isn't as smart as them. Who isn't as rich as them. Who isn't as male as them."

"Not as male?" I said.

"We're at the bottom of the shit list, Russo. Women."

"But women are on the board," I said. "What about all the wives or mothers over the years? What about you?"

"Me? Think I'm different because I'm an Abbott? I'm a female. We're here to wait on the men and fuck for the men. That clear enough?" She took a drink of wine and put the glass down. "We've learned our roles all too well, I'm afraid."

"That's a pretty harsh assessment."

"Not as harsh as my father deserves. Certainly not as harsh as my brother deserves."

I noticed that more tables in the front room were busy with happy people, enjoying good food and good conversation. Less so at this end of the bar.

"My information about Cherokee Point was not that specific," I said.

"I'll bet," Parker said. But just that quickly, her face brightened, her eyes opened wider. Like she'd come out of deep thought. "So what kind of man are you, Russo? Huh?"

She leaned in again. "You know, I could make it easier for you to see my boobs." She put her index fingers at the top button of her blouse and played with the edges of it. She smiled.

"Sorry," I said.

She sat up. "Don't be sorry, for crissake. Don't be deferential to me, goddamn it. Drag me out of here and make love to me." She drank some wine and wiped a drop from the corner of her mouth. "As long as we're discussing fucking," she laughed, "keep fucking with The Fraternity, will ya? Especially my brother. Somebody has to." Her mood changed again. She was angry. "Gave it my best shot. Where'd it get me? Didn't get me shit. Too many of 'em. One of 'em's gone, there's always more."

"You talking about Nick?"

"Jesus, Russo," she said. "Pay attention. I'm giving you the inside scoop on the vaunted Cherokee Point." I thought she was about to get up and leave, but she settled herself on the stool and reached for her wine. She drank more. "They're all nasty men, especially to women. Nick's the ugliest, that's all. You must have cotton in your head? Maybe I oughta blow you right here, right now. Clear your head. Men. They're like snakes. You know, cut the head off and another head is always there, always . . ." There was a sadness in her face. In her eyes. I thought for a moment she might cry.

I was wrong.

Parker Abbott leaned in and undid the top button of her blouse. With her right finger, she pulled one half of the blouse open just enough to show a cherry-red lace bra.

"Go ahead," she said. "I want you to look. We get oughta here, I'll take my clothes off. Just for you. Slowly. I'll start with this," she said and moved her hand to her skirt. She hiked her skirt up an inch. "No panties. No thong. Should get you hard enough. Thinking about that." She smiled. "But if it doesn't, I'll get rid of all the clothes."

Parker sat up, picked up her wine and drank. The glass was almost empty again. She leaned back in. "I give a world-class blow job, Russo. If you can last long enough. See, I start slow and easy. Mouth and tongue.

When you start to twitch, when your hips can't help themselves, I'll finish you off. Suck every drop."

She sat up and drank the rest of the wine. "What d'ya say, let's get outta here. If you can walk." She laughed.

"Thanks," I said, "for the flattering offer. Sounds like fun." I drank wine from my nearly empty glass. "I like oral sex as much as the next guy." I cleared my throat. "It's fun and all, but, you know." I shrugged. "Get that a lot, actually."

Parker's smile was gone. She cocked her head to one side. "The newspaper woman? Lester?"

I nodded.

"She wouldn't have to know, Russo." The smile reappeared. "You could do a little comparison shopping. My tongue, her tongue. I won't tell, if you won't tell."

I'd trust her about as far as I could toss a sports car.

"I'm committed to A.J. Lester, Parker. Like it that way."

"Really?"

"Yeah," I said. "I like my life the way it is. I . . ."

"Your life," Parker said, hard.

I nodded.

"That's all you think about, isn't it? Your life." She was angry again. "You're just like all of them, Russo. You know that? Your life. What about my life? Huh?"

This was headed downhill, fast. "Parker," I said, trying to lower the heat. "Your friends are having fun down there." I gestured at her companions.

Parker shook her head. "Just like the rest of them. You men." Her voice was hard, defiant. "You use me, you . . . you draw me in, then . . ."

My gut said do nothing, say nothing. I didn't listen. "Parker, you introduced yourself to me, wanted to have a drink."

"Same shit my father used to pull. I've had it with you, too." With that she stood up. She grabbed the bar to steady herself, knocking over the wine glass. Her companions all looked our way. "I'm oughta here," she said. She turned and walked away, not as steadily as she arrived. She went right past her friends and around the end of the bar. They watched her go by.

Over the shoulder of the redhead, the one with the halter-top and tanned skin, I spotted A.J. at the door. Parker stopped, she exchanged words with A.J., then left. A.J. came around the end of the bar. The three women watched her as she came up to me and kissed me lightly on the lips.

"Good evening, darling." She smiled. "Did we have fun waiting?" she said and sat down on the same stool recently vacated by Parker Abbott.

36

Meg appeared in front of us. "Good evening, Ms. Lester," she said, "What can I get you?"

"You drinking Chardonnay?"

I nodded.

"Me, too," she said to Meg.

"Be right back," Meg said.

"Been standing there long?"

"Long enough to get a feel for the conversation. So to speak."

I nodded. "What did Parker say to you, anyway?"

"I believe Ms. Abbott mentioned oral sex," A.J. said, with a wry smile on her face.

"Really."

A.J. nodded. "Of course, those weren't her exact words." Meg put a glass of wine and a coaster on the bar. A.J. took a sip and looked up, as if trying to recall a long lost thought. "I'll need all my experience as a trained reporter here."

"You enjoying this?" I said.

"You bet," she said. "Parker Abbott said and I quote, 'you must give good head, lady.'"

"To which you replied?"

"I said, quote, 'I do and often.'"

"That when she turned on her heels and left?"

"Yep."

"Well," I said, "it's been a while since a woman tried to seduce me."

"What d'ya mean?" A.J. said, trying to sound indignant, "I seduced you the other night." She picked up her glass. "Don't remember if I said anything about giving head, but walking into the living room with no clothes on while you were watching Chris Matthews worked just fine." She sipped some Chardonnay and ate a piece of cheese.

"Very funny," I said.

"Thank you, darling."

We were quiet for a minute. I grabbed the last piece of cheese, put it with a cracker and popped into my mouth. A.J. got Meg's attention and she refilled the wine glass.

"You know," I said, "getting noticed by an attractive woman can be flattering, but," I shook my head, "not this time. Not flattering and certainly not fun."

"Too much wine?"

"Maybe," I said, "but she flashed back and forth between seduction and anger."

"Mad at you for turning her down?"

"Yeah," I said, "wouldn't do what she wanted. That came after nasty comments about her father and, particularly, her brother." I reached for another piece of cheese, then realized it was gone. "Nasty comments about men, generally."

A.J. nodded her head.

"What?"

"When Parker stopped on her way out? Before we discussed blow jobs? She made a couple of cracks about men. Like, 'had enough' or 'they're all alike.' Like that. Lots of anger there."

I nodded. "Makes me wonder," I said.

"About what?"

"The words were angry, sure, but it was the feel of it, the way she said it. Felt more like rage to me."

"Think she's capable of more than words?"

"Could be," I said. "Rage is a whole lot different than angry."

"You're not thinking . . ." A.J. lowered her voice. Almost a whisper. "You're not thinking about her father, are you?"

"Big stretch, I know, but who else?" I said. "What do you think?"

"Very big stretch," she said, "but rage is a dangerous animal."

"Think he might be on to something?"

"Kelsey Sheridan?" she said.

I nodded.

"Big stretch."

A few tables had turned over since I sat down. Still a slow night at the City Park Grill. A.J. put her hand on my knee. I looked at her and smiled. "Want to get a sandwich here?" I said.

A.J. shook her head. "Got a great batch of chili in the fridge. That okay?"

"Yes, it is." I started to move from my stool, but A.J. squeezed my leg.

"What was it Parker Abbott said to you? Exactly." She smiled.

I told her.

"No panties?"

"What she said."

"Hmm. Guess I'll have to take mine off when we get home. The little black lacy ones?" A.J. slid her hand up my leg, stopping at the top of my thigh. "Or you could take them off."

"Be my pleasure."

37

"Stay here much longer, we'll fall asleep," I said. A.J.'s head was on my shoulder, my arm was around her. Our legs were tangled up some way or other.

"I know," she said. "Don't wanna move."

"Me either," I said. "You stay and I'll warm up the chili."

A.J. nodded without lifting her head off my shoulder. "Wonder if good ole Parker has a better technique?"

"Enough, already," I said.

"Not what you said a few minutes ago."

"A.J."

"Okay, okay." She sat up and dropped the sheet. "One last look before I get in the shower."

"Thank you," I said.

A.J. got out of bed and went down the hall to the bathroom. I heard the shower come on. I put on my boxers and took a pair of running pants from a hook in the closet. I got a sweatshirt from the shelf above the hanger rack and put it on. It said "Made in Detroit" across the front.

While I warmed the chili the old-fashioned way, in a pan on the stove, I tore up some Romaine lettuce, chopped a large tomato, two green onions, and threw in a few slices of cucumber. I mixed some Italian spices with red wine vinegar and olive oil from Fustini's.

A.J. came into the kitchen wrapped in a fluffy white terrycloth robe. Her hair was still wet. She looked wonderful. But I always thought that.

"You look wonderful," I said.

"You always think that, darling, but thank you."

"You're welcome."

"I'm pretty hungry," she said. "Want to eat in the living room?"

"Sure," I said. "Chili's almost ready."

A.J. took silverware and napkins to the coffee table. She got two wine glasses. "Did you open any wine?" I shook my head. She went to the fridge and took out a bottle and opened it.

"Sauvignon Blanc okay?"

"Sure." I tossed the salad and put it in bowls and ladled two large helpings of chili. "Here you go," I said.

We sat at the coffee table. "Good chili," I said.

"Thanks." A.J. put down her spoon and looked at me. "When the Abbott case is over, how about a couple of days in Chicago? What do you say?"

"I say, yes. Can you get away from the paper?"

A.J. nodded. "I'll talk to Maury," she said. "It'll work if I can flex the days."

We sat quietly and enjoyed the food, the wine and being together.

"Michael," A.J. said. "About Parker and her father."

I put down my chili bowl. "Yes?"

"Are you reacting with your head or your gut?"

"Gut," I said without hesitation. "Head still says DeMio. Less sure now." I stopped eating, picked up my wine glass and sat back on the couch. "What about you?"

"I don't know. I really don't." A.J. poured herself more wine and tipped the bottle in my direction. I shook my head.

"You still going to meet with Frank and Sheridan?"

I nodded. "Kelsey's in. Sandy's waiting to hear from Frank."

"Good. Be interesting what they say now that you're open to other suggestions."

"Yes, it will."

38

I was on my second cup of coffee when A.J. came into the kitchen.

"Pour me a cup, will you. I have to finish my makeup." She looked at her watch. "I've got an editorial board meeting in a few minutes."

I handed her a mug. She swallowed some and said, "You're not dressed. Not going to the office?"

"Yeah, but no early appointments." I dropped an English muffin into the toaster. "Want half?"

"No time," A.J. said. "I'll run over to Julienne Tomatoes and grab a bagel." She left for the bathroom, only to return a few minutes later, makeup all done. She drank some coffee.

"By the way, Sandy called," I said. "I'm meeting Sheridan and Marshall for lunch."

"Where?"

"Wanted the Twisted Olive, but Sandy thought it too small and too public for a lively discussion about murder."

"Smart woman," A.J. said.

"We'll get sandwiches or salads. Eat in the office."

"Sandy gonna sit in?" A.J. said.

"Yes, she is."

A.J. looked at her watch again. "Gotta go." She grabbed her briefcase off the floor. She gave me a light kiss and said, "Let's go to the Island Friday. I can get away early. I'll ride my bike. You do a long run. What do you say?"

"Good idea," I said. "I'll get a place to stay. See you tonight?"

She threw a jacket over her arm. "Don't plan on it. Be a long day. I'll call later. Bye."

I put some orange marmalade on the muffin and sat at the kitchen table with more coffee. Wonder what Kelsey Sheridan will have to say when he finds out I'm taking him seriously. Or what Frank Marshall will have to say about any of it.

I drank the last of my coffee, put the dishes in the dishwasher and went to take a shower. I put on jeans and dark green polo shirt. Might as well be comfortable. I took a black fleece jacket, picked up my bag and went out the door.

I walked up Howard and cut across the parking lot to Mclean & Eakin to pick up my *New York Times*.

"Good late morning, Michael," Sandy said when I entered the office. It was a little after ten.

"Funny lady," I said.

Sandy shook her head. "That was Streisand," she said. "Lousy movie."

"Really?"

Sandy nodded. "Roger Ebert called it a 'messy flop.' Me, too. Your mail's on the desk."

I hung up my jacket and put my brief bag down at my desk. Sandy came in and sat down.

"Marshall and Sheridan'll be here about one," she said. "What do you want to do about food?"

"Wait until they get here and we'll order carry out from Roast & Toast."

"You must be serious about this Sheridan thing if we're doing a round table discussion."

"We'll see," I said. "Call the Cloghaun. See if they've got a room for Friday. A.J. and I are going up for the night."

"Okay," Sandy said and left.

I made a few notes ahead of our lunch meeting. Would Sheridan push his theory harder knowing that I was more open to it? More important, I wanted to know what the experienced investigator had to say. Too bad I didn't buy those private eye novels last night. Sure could use some tips from the pros.

"**G**entlemen," Sandy said as she put down two large plastic bags filled with sandwiches and salads. "Our food has arrived."

"We're on a first name basis here," I said.

"That's fine," Frank said. "Kelsey, I've known you a long time and it's nice this won't be more small talk."

"Resort speak," Kelsey said. "Keep it innocuous. Keep it simple. Keep out of trouble."

"Heard that one before," Frank said.

I opened my egg wrap and took a bite.

"Since this is my show," I said. "Kelsey, would you tell Frank and Sandy what you think about Carleton Abbott's death? The original version, the one you told me."

"Be glad to," he said. "You understand, this is how I'd write it for a novel. Never supposed to be real." Marshall nodded. For the next ten minutes, Sheridan highlighted his theory of Abbott's murder.

"Of course," Sheridan said, "subsequent events have altered my plot line, so to speak."

"Such as?" Marshall said.

"Well, my theory's based on Parker's almost pathological hatred for her father. That hasn't changed. But Parker's plan to cleverly pin it on either her brother or boyfriend didn't work out so well."

"Joey's still suspect number one," Marshall said.

Sheridan nodded. "That keeps Parker out of prison, but doesn't get her any of Daddy's money, property or business interests. Nick gets it all. Parker gets the shaft."

"If she's the killer and Joey takes the fall, she gets away with murder," Marshall said. "That's quite a feat."

"Sure is," Sheridan said. "But if that's all she gets, my theory's dead on arrival."

"Unless she killed for revenge," Sandy said. "Suppose there never was another motive. Money or property. Suppose it was to get back at her father?"

"She killed him to get even? Nothing else?" Sheridan shook his head. "Not enough motive."

"If it was fueled by rage, it would be," I said.

"You think so?" Sheridan said.

"You said it yourself, Kelsey. Something like 'could hate be so strong it leads to murder.'"

"Look," Sheridan said, "it's nice you guys believe that my fictional plot could be that real, but I'm in over my head here. This isn't a plot for a mystery novel anymore."

"Why do you think it was rage, Michael?" Marshall said.

I told them about my evening at the City Park Grill, about my reaction and A.J.'s comments.

"All that and oral sex, too?"

"Sandy," I said, "for Pete's sake."

She shrugged. "Just asking."

"But too much alcohol and sex talk in a bar is thin evidence of murder, Michael," Marshall said.

"By itself, sure," I said, "but add that to Kelsey's plot and it looks different." I leaned forward on my desk. "Remember, Kelsey's playing inside baseball here. He knows Cherokee Point and the people better than we do." I glanced at Sheridan. So did Marshall.

"Lived there all my life," he said. "Frank, you've been there, what, ten years or so?"

Marshall nodded.

"It's not the same. I grew up with them. Parker, Nick. You learn it differently as a kid. You feel it differently. When I was ten years old, I knew Parker hated her father."

"Why, Kelsey? Why'd she hate him?" Marshall said.

Sheridan sat back in his chair and stared at his salad. He looked up at me. Not the confident novelist anymore.

"Kelsey," I said, "tell us what you know separate from what you think."

Sheridan looked around the room, at each of us. "Okay. Parker hated her father. When we'd be alone, I mean kids, no adults, she'd yell or scream at him like he was there. Happened all the time. She'd cry a lot, too. If one of us tried to help or asked what was wrong, she'd push us away. Or yell at us." Sheridan picked up his water and drank some. "When we were in high school, we'd drink beer late at night, on the beach. Same thing. She'd yell or cry. It happened after we went off to college, too. Dragged her out of the Side Door more than once when it got too loud. She yelled at the bartender one night because he put two olives in her Martini instead of one." He gestured at me. "She acted the same way with you and Ms. Lester."

I nodded.

"Some kids hate their parents," Marshall said. "Or say they do. They get over it."

"Not if she was raped." It was Sandy. We all looked at her. "Not if it started when she was a kid." There were tears in the corner of her eyes. "You don't get over that." She looked down. A few tears dropped onto the yellow legal pad in her lap. She took a deep breath and raised her head. "Not without professional help you don't."

I put a Kleenex box on the corner of the desk. Sandy took one and nodded a thank you. She was crying softly.

"Sandy?" I said.

"I'm a survivor, Michael." She dabbed her eyes and blew her nose. "It was a long time ago."

"You never said anything."

"I'm one of the lucky ones. I got help. Damn good thing my husband had insurance. I didn't have to tell you, Michael, because I've learned how to live with my past, how to manage it."

"That mean you've gotten past it?" I said.

"Put it in the past," she said, "along side all the good things in the past. I've adjusted to the consequences of it. Do it every day."

"Sandy," Marshall said, "I'm sorry."

"Thank you."

"Do you think Parker Abbott was abused by her father?" Marshall said.

Sandy took a drink of water. "Here's what I'm comfortable saying. Kelsey described Parker's behavior as a child, a teenager, a young adult. Michael described her similar behavior now. We know things about her life from the police report. Smart woman but never had a real career. Lots of jobettes. She'd take off for California or some damn place to find herself. Never did. Then there's sex. It's a manipulative device. Gets her attention from men and it gets men to do what she wants them to do."

"All that adds up to, what?" Marshall said.

"It adds up to the life of a survivor who never got professional help. Do I know, for sure, she was raped by her father? No. But every time I hear a story like that? Every time, I react the same way, Frank. Every time."

I rubbed my face with my hands. It didn't help. The tension in the room had eased, but we all knew that the case of Carleton Abbott's death had taken a sad and ugly turn if Sandy Jeffries was right.

"One thing I know," I said, "Joey DeMio is no longer the only suspect."

"Devil's advocate, Michael?" Marshall said.

"Go ahead."

"You believe Parker Abbott shot her father, Michael?"

"Didn't say that, Frank. But we have another plausible suspect. She had plenty of opportunities to kill him."

"What about a gun?"

"Not a problem," Sheridan said. "Lot of guns on the Point. Every guy, especially the older ones, thinks he's John Wayne." Sheridan pointed at Marshall, "I'll anticipate your next question. Doors are unlocked. It's a silly attempt to pretend they live in a land filled with apple pie, soda fountains and trustworthy people. Nineteenth century America."

"Okay. That still leaves motive, Michael. A lot of survivors of sexual abuse don't kill their perpetrators. Why is it a good enough motive here?"

"Frank, I don't know if it's good enough or not. But I do know that Kelsey kept the idea of another killer afloat. Sandy's educated guesses about Parker mean we can't assume Joey DeMio's the killer."

Sandy's eyes were dry, but she stared out the window at Little Traverse Bay. Hard to tell what she was thinking.

40

"I feel so bad for Sandy," A.J. said. "I can't imagine living with that."

"Me either," I said, "but recovering from the past is most important. That was clear listening to her this afternoon."

"I guess."

We sat in my kitchen, at the small café table. I'd washed the car on the way home, then did a short run. Both helped ease the tension. I was staring into the refrigerator when A.J. called to say she was leaving work. Told her I didn't feel like eating out, that I'd fix something.

"Glad you got done early," I said. "It's especially good to see you right now."

"I know," she said and touched my cheek.

"The omelet okay?" I'd chopped up some tomato and green onion and sautéed them. When the eggs started to set, I added the vegetables and some cheddar slices. I put two English muffins in the toaster and orange marmalade and raspberry preserves on the table. I open a bottle of Chardonnay and set it on the table with two glasses.

"The omelet is delicious, darling." A.J. leaned over and kissed me. "Very sweet of you to make dinner."

"I never guessed about Sandy," I said.

"No reason you would. She's made a good life for herself."

"But she said she deals with it every day."

"Sure, but in a healthy way, a recovering way," A.J. said. "Big difference from someone like Parker Abbott. If she's right about her."

My phone buzzed on the kitchen counter. I reached behind me and picked it up. "It's Sandy."

"Hey," I said. I listened. "Okay . . . Uh-huh . . . Got it . . . How you doing, by the way? . . . Nice to hear. Thanks."

"How she doing?"

"Pretty good, she said. Got a glass of Merlot, watching the Tigers."

A.J. smiled. "What'd she want?"

"Cloghaun's full. Got us a room at the Windermere. On the French Lane side." I took the last bite of my omelet. "With everything else this afternoon, she forgot to tell me."

I picked up our plates and put them in the sink. "More wine?" A.J. nodded and I filled our glasses. "What were you saying about Parker?"

"Well, big difference between a survivor who's recovering and one who isn't. That's all."

"Sandy and Parker."

"Uh-huh." A.J. sipped her wine. "Seems to me you got a problem."

"Which is?"

"The double alibi . . . Joey for Parker, Parker for Joey. What'd you do with that?"

I turned on the water in the sink, rinsed the dishes and put them in the dishwasher. A.J. nodded towards the living room. We took our wine and sat on the couch.

"If Parker's the killer, they're both lying. Hendricks and Fleener are convinced Parker's not telling the truth, but not because of this. Joey could be lying through his teeth, but he's had more experience with the cops than she has."

"They gonna talk to Parker again?"

"Yeah," I said, "this time not at home."

"Money has its privileges."

"Yes, it does." I put my legs on the coffee table and leaned back with my hands behind my head. "What time can you get away tomorrow?"

"By one, I imagine," A.J. said. "I'll throw some things in a bag tonight. I'll put the bike in my car and pick you up. Oughta be at the dock in Mac City by two-thirty."

"It's a truck," I said.

"It's an SUV," A.J. said slowly.

"They're all trucks."

"Snob," she said. "Just because you drive a sports car . . ."

"Sports sedan," I said. "A BMW is a sports sedan."

"You are impossible about cars." A.J. stood up. "Kiss me goodnight will you. Gotta go pack."

I stood up, put my arms around her waist and pulled her to me. I pressed hard against her as we kissed.

"Feels good. Pick you up after one," she said and waved good-bye.

I pushed the cork back into the bottle and put it in the refrigerator. I rinsed our glasses and added them to the dishwasher.

Joey and Parker. Who would let go of the alibi first? My money's on the amateur.

41

"**Y**ou bring rain gear?" A.J. said.

"Silly question, my love, silly question. This is Northern Michigan."

"Uh-huh," she said, "you bring it?"

"Running gear and a regular rain parka. Happy now?"

A.J. smiled.

"Besides, it's not going to rain. Clouds'll blow out in an hour or two."

We sat on the lower deck of the three-thirty Catamaran as it pulled away from the dock in Mackinaw City. Every time I cross the Straits, I feel the same way. The majesty of the Mackinac Bridge and that first close-up of the harbor on Mackinac Island. Spectacular sights.

The Cat cut its engines when we came around the west breakwall. It eased up to the dock. Out the side window, I saw two familiar figures near the top of the ramp.

Henri LaCroix. Santino Cicci. Not twenty feet apart.

"Recognize the two men on the dock?"

"Don't think so," A.J. said, "Who are they."

"One on the left, jeans and tan jacket, is Henri LaCroix."

"So that's LaCroix," she said. "Think he's waiting for us?"

"If he's not, the other one is."

"Who's that?"

"Santino Cicci, gunslinger for Carmine DeMio."

"Really?" A.J. said. "Waiting for us?"

"Find out soon enough."

The deck hands tied the Cat to the dock and dropped the ramp. LaCroix moved closer. Cicci did not. We followed the luggage carts off the ferry and moved away from the rest of the passengers.

"Mr. Russo," LaCroix said. "Nice to see you again." We shook hands. "Ms. Lester? Pleased to meet you." He reached out his hand.

"Call me A.J." As they shook hands, she said, "I'm delighted to meet the man who shows up when he's needed."

"Do we need you, Henri?" I said, nodding towards Cicci.

LaCroix took a few steps towards Cicci. "A.J., this is Mr. Santino Cicci. He's here to follow the two of you. I'm here to follow him following you. Make sure he plays nice." LaCroix smiled broadly. "Isn't that right, Santino?"

Cicci folded his arms across his chest and leaned against the soft drink machine. He said nothing.

"Come on, man," LaCroix said. "Island's a small place. They'll see your tail. Especially in that cheap suit. Lose the tie. Get some shorts and a sweatshirt, for crissake." We picked up our bags from the luggage cart, LaCroix took A.J.'s bike and we headed up the dock to Main Street.

"Santino," I said, as we walked by him, "checking in at the Windermere. Walk around a while. Dinner at the Jockey Club. That make it easier?"

An empty horse-drawn dray turned onto the dock as we got to the street. LaCroix nodded at the driver. "Henri," he said in return.

A.J. said, "I'll ride my bike to the hotel. Meet you there in few minutes."

"Okay," I said, and LaCroix and I started down the sidewalk.

"You knew we were coming?"

"Got people on the dock in the City. St. Ignace, too. So does DeMio."

I looked up Astor Street as we went by. Saw the sign for Fran Warren's Sandal Company. "Fran on the island?"

"Probably in the store."

"You two want to join us for dinner?" I said.

"I'll make reservations at seven," he said. "Jockey Club, right?"

"Right. Think we can get in this late?"

"We'll get in," he said.

With that, I expected LaCroix to head somewhere else. He didn't.

"Where you going?" I said.

"Windermere Hotel," he said.

We kept walking. "Why?"

"Nice place," he said. "Like the sun room."

"That's not what I meant."

LaCroix stopped. Me, too. We were in front of the Lilac Tree Hotel. "We've had this talk before, Russo. Nothing's changed."

"You really think Cicci will start something on the street?"

"Don't know. That's why I'm going to the Windermere." He gestured at the hotel's courtyard shops. "Could get a newspaper at the Island Bookstore. To read in the sunroom."

"Funny. You gonna follow me for twenty-four hours?"

"Uh-huh." We started down the sidewalk again.

"What about A.J.?" I said.

"They're not interested in her."

"You sure?"

"You're the troublemaker, Russo."

"Don't think of myself as a troublemaker," I said.

"Carmine DeMio thinks so."

"You armed?"

"Armed?" he said. "On Mackinac Island? What could happen here?"

"Learn that smart-ass banter in Blackwater?"

LaCroix glanced sideways. "Learned lots of things in Blackwater, Russo. Most you don't want to know."

"Got a few questions," I said.

"Another time."

We arrived at the Windermere Hotel. Built in 1887 as a private cottage on Windermere Point, it was converted into a hotel by Robert Doud at the start of the twentieth century. Even with the addition of a third floor and the sunroom, the Windermere kept the charm of a boutique hotel.

We started up the walk as A.J. came down the steps.

"All checked in," she said. "Got two keys. Bike's over there." She pointed to the bike rack just inside the fence.

"Henri and Fran are going to join us for dinner."

"Terrific," A.J. said. "Did you see Fran?"

LaCroix shook his head. "She's working, but we'd be happy to tag along."

My cell chirped. I took it from my pocket. "Gotta take it," I said, "it's Don Hendricks." I went into the front yard, away from other people.

I swiped the phone, "Hello, Don," I said. "What's up?"

As I listened to Hendricks, I saw Santino Cicci across the street, sitting at a picnic table at the Doghouse snack bar. He wasn't eating a hotdog.

"Okay, Don," I said. "Thanks for calling. Appreciate it." I went back to A.J. and LaCroix. "We have company," I said, gesturing at Cicci. Both of them turned to look.

"Think he's gonna be with us all the time?" A.J. said.

Neither of us answered. Didn't have to.

"What'd Hendricks want, Michael?"

"Joey DeMio's flying from LA," I said. "They'll arrest him when he changes planes in Detroit."

"Charge him with Abbott's murder?" LaCroix said.

I nodded. "Hendricks promised he'd give me a heads up. Got three hours before the flight lands in Pellston. Time enough to see Carmine."

"Think he needs to hear about Joey from you, Michael?" A.J. said.

"I want him to," I said. "Can't tell you why, but I do." I looked at LaCroix. "Henri . . ."

"He's on the Island," LaCroix said. He glanced at his watch. "Late afternoon, probably at the house."

"You know for sure?"

"It's my business to know, Russo. He's there."

"What's the best way?" I said. "Just walk up and knock on the door?"

LaCroix jerked his hand, hitchhiker style, over his shoulder. "Cicci." Santino Cicci was still enjoying the accommodations at the Doghouse.

I started across the street. LaCroix came up behind me. "Where you going?"

"Get a hotdog," he said.

No point arguing. Cicci stiffened as we came up, but he didn't move off the bench. His suit coat was buttoned.

"I want to talk to your boss," I said.

No response.

"Call Carmine, tell him I want ten minutes. It's important or I wouldn't ask."

No response.

"Santino," LaCroix said. "Two choices. Call Carmine like the man said or I'll go up there and kick the door in."

"You'd never make it through the door," Cicci said.

LaCroix sat down on the bench next to Cicci and smiled. "A word of caution, Santino. You get a hotdog, maybe chips, at the snack bar," he said, pointing at the kiosk next to the picnic table, "don't put 'em down. Seagulls. Take 'em right off the table. Call your boss, Santino."

Cicci stood up slowly, pulled out a phone and walked towards the water. Three seagulls flew around over our heads. He made the call.

Cicci came back to me and said, "Mr. DeMio's expecting you." He looked at LaCroix. "Not you, tough guy."

"Whatever you say, Santino, whatever you say."

I went back to tell A.J. "Sure you'll be okay?" she said.

I nodded. "Just want him to hear it from me."

"Something about the man got to you didn't it?"

"Yeah," I said. "I'll meet you back here."

I started up the sidewalk towards the park. Cicci came quickly from across the street. LaCroix followed.

When they got close enough, Cicci said to LaCroix, "Russo goes alone."

"How about you and me tag along," LaCroix said. "Talk about Island history, cuisine, that sorta thing?" No response from Cicci. "Russo goes in alone. We wait outside for him to come out. Deal?" Cicci nodded and we were off.

The sidewalks were crowded with visitors checking the store displays, reading menus taped in restaurant windows. "Watch the horses, please. Turning right," a driver shouted. A few tourists scattered out of the way as a taxi filled with visitors and luggage turned up Astor Street. It's a perennial problem on the island: too many visitors forget that a pair of two thousand pound horses outweighs the family sedan.

I moved around people waiting for the next tour carriage to leave for its sightseeing run. By the time I got to the park, LaCroix and Cicci were in lock step, twenty feet behind me. I stopped and waited for them at Doud's corner.

"Which way, Santino?" I said. "Stairs in the park or Church Street?" Cicci pointed straight head. That meant Church Street, so we kept walking. I glanced at the front porch of the Marquette Park Hotel as we went by. Did I expect to see Gino Rosato with a shotgun on the front porch? Must be nervous. This meeting was my idea, so why be nervous? Because I'm about to tell a retired Mafia Don that his son will be arrested for murder.

The sidewalks were less congested as we moved away from the shops and restaurants. Children ran around the park, yelling, having fun. Some people, mostly teens, sat on the steps at Père Marquette's statue, reading or soaking up the sun. A few boats bounced gently in their slips in the marina. It was less than half full. Normal for this time of year.

In a few minutes we turned up Church Street at Ste. Anne's Church and headed for stairs at the base of the East Bluff. It was up hill now and the stairs were steep, but none of us broke stride.

DeMio's house, still called the Brewster cottage, waited for us at the top of the stairs. Built in 1892 by Matt Elliott for H. L. Jenness, the cottage featured a huge wrap around porch that faced south and east and captured the morning sun. The exterior shingles were stained a deep brown and white.

Ignoring a rickety stairway that twisted and turned its way up to the porch, Cicci said, "That way," and pointed to a grass covered walk next to the side yard. "The back door," he said, "you'll see it." He turned to LaCroix and said, "We'll wait right here, tough guy. He won't be long."

I went up the grass walk and behind the house. Tucked into the trees was a small porch. The door opened as I arrived at the porch.

"Mr. Russo," the man said, "I'm Carlo Vollini, Mr. DeMio's secretary." He stepped aside. "Come in, please." Didn't look like the secretaries who met for drinks at Chandler's or the City Park Grill. He was big, maybe six-six and two-thirty. He wore tan cord pants and a royal blue V-neck sweater that pushed tight against his stomach.

We were in a small kitchen that missed its update in the 1950s.

"This way," Vollini said and I followed him through a short hallway into a large dining room at the front of the house. Small paned windows covered the front wall and looked out on the harbor. A long, dark wooden table sat in the center of the room. At the far end of the table stood Carmine DeMio. He wore freshly creased faded jeans and a black blazer over a white shirt. No tie. Resort casual. I expected an offer to sit down. I was wrong. I went over to him and stopped, about six feet away. Vollini waited in the corner by the windows.

"Thank you for seeing me, Mr. DeMio."

"Okay. Get to it. What do you want?"

"I'm still helping the cops on the Abbott murder."

"Bully for you. You got more questions?"

"No."

"What then?"

"Cops got a new suspect. Wanted to tell you myself."

"Uh-huh."

"It's Joey."

"Nothing new about that. Joey's been a suspect ever since . . ." He hesitated. "What are you telling me?"

"Cops arrested him. Met his plane in Detroit. Fleener will get him at Pellston in a couple of hours. Wanted to tell you myself."

DeMio said nothing. He didn't move, but he put his hand out on a tall, wingback chair to steady himself.

"Got himself messed up with the Abbotts." DeMio shook his head. "Tried to tell him those people were trouble." For a brief moment he almost seemed sad, introspective. He recovered quickly. His body straightened, he put his arms out, hands on his hips. "Carlo," he said. Vollini nodded and left the room.

"Our lawyer will be in Petoskey by the time the cops bring Joey in. You shouldda left things alone, Russo. You stirred things up from the start."

"It wasn't me," I said, "and you know it. A dead body brings the cops every time."

"Joey's got friends won't like what you did, Russo."

"Come on, Carmine, you said it yourself. They'd come after you. Sooner or later, but they'd come."

DeMio said nothing.

"Well," I said, "thanks for seeing me." I put my hands in my pockets and went for the door.

"Russo."

I looked back.

"Why?"

"Why what?"

"Why'd you want to tell me? I'd find out soon enough."

"Respect. The day we met at the hotel. Remember?"

DeMio nodded.

"You listened to what I had to say. When I told you to call off your goons." I shrugged. "Besides, Joey's your son. He's a gangster, but he's still your kid."

I went back through the kitchen and out the door. LaCroix and Cicci were standing at the side of the road. They looked up as I came down the grassy walk. I stopped at the road. I turned to LaCroix. "Let's go."

42

We walked up the road, passing the cottages that overlooked the Straits. Most of the houses were updated to survive more than a hundred years of life in a tough climate. A few had been rebuilt, but one redo was so gaudy, it was like too much make-up on a woman old enough to know better.

"No smart comments, LaCroix."

"Don't get pissed at me, Russo," he said. "Figured you'd say something when you were ready."

"Sorry," I said. "It's just . . . I had to tell him. That's all."

"Maybe it's not worth thinking about."

"Maybe not," I said. "Let's take the stairs," I said, pointing into the woods in front of the Sawyer cottage. We made our way down the long stairway that ran behind the Yacht Club and the Marquette Park Hotel. We cut across the park to Market Street.

"All I got for my trouble was a threat. Said Joey's friends would hold me responsible for his arrest."

"Joey's got no friends," LaCroix said, "unless they work for Carmine."

"Meaning?"

"Meaning you'll get trouble if Carmine orders it," he said. "But that's why I showed up. Keep the boys honest."

We stopped in front of the Community Hall. LaCroix pointed down Astor Street. "I'll tell Fran she's got plans for dinner. Think you can stay out of trouble for a while?"

"Do my best," I said. "See you later."

I went down Hoban past the Village Inn to the Windermere. A.J. was napping in a lounge chair in the front window of our room. She stirred when I closed the door.

"Tried to be quiet," I said.

"That's okay," A.J. said. "Gotta take a shower pretty soon anyway."

I leaned down and kissed her. "Nice," she said. She took my hand and kissed it. I sat down in the other chair.

"Everything okay?"

"Yeah," I said. "Told him about Joey. He wasn't happy."

"You expected something else?"

I shook my head. "Of course not. It was important to tell him myself."

"It's not worth thinking about," she said.

"That what LaCroix said."

"That reminds me." A.J. looked at the clock on the dresser. "It's getting late." She got up. "I'll be in the shower if you feel compelled to stare," she said and laughed.

"Be my pleasure," I said. I heard the water come on. I stood at the window. Across the street, at the same picnic table as before, sat Santino Cicci.

43

"**Y**ou two know the Island better than we do," A.J. said, looking across the table at Fran Warren and Henri LaCroix. "Do locals simply tolerate DeMio and his men?"

We sat at the center table inside the Jockey Club. It's across the road from Grand Hotel, at the golf course. It's a small, intimate restaurant with enough atmosphere for several visits. A large, heavy mahogany bar runs the length of one wall and a fireplace sits on another wall. Only a few tables are spread around the room.

We'd ordered a bottle of the house Chardonnay. A.J. picked up her glass and drank some. "Do they do this to other people? Follow 'em around?"

"He's the only one right now," LaCroix said, pointing at me.

"That's not reassuring," A.J. said.

"Maybe not," LaCroix said, "but ever since Michael told Carmine to lay off the citizenry, it's gotten better." He put down his menu. "Cicci and Rosato have kept to themselves more. Don't hassle locals as much."

"You're welcome, Henri," I said. "Glad to help."

"Ladies and gentlemen," our server said in a distinctly Jamaican accent, "have we decided?" He was tall, six-five maybe, thin and dressed in black pants and black tie with a short white jacket.

"I'm ready," Fran Warren said. "Whitefish please."

"Me, too," A.J. said. LaCroix ordered the strip steak, rare and I ordered the duck.

"Think DeMio's really lightened up?" Fran asked her brother.

"Time will tell," he said. "Haven't spotted Cicci tonight."

"He's here," I said. I sat facing the side window. "He's in the tent." Off to the side of the restaurant, next to the golf club's pro shop was a large white tent, the "Light House," for smokers. "Saw him come up the sidewalk."

"Maybe he'll choke," Fran said.

"He hasn't let up," A.J. said.

I reached for another roll. "Pass me the butter, please." A.J. handed me the small dish.

LaCroix said, "Cicci knew you'd be here. No need to sit with the smokers. They're sticking to the plan, such as it is."

"I'm sure they are," I said, "but there was a moment there, when I told Carmine about his son." I leaned forward, on my elbows. "The façade cracked. Just a bit, but I saw it. He told me that he'd warned Joey about the Abbotts, about . . ."

"Hold on a second," A.J. said, "you mean to tell me that a Mafia Don from Chicago is scared by a bunch of guys who wear apple green sweaters and drink too much?"

"No, that's not what I'm saying."

"Then what, Michael?" Fran said.

Our server arrived with plates of food. I sipped my wine and waited while he placed our dinners on the table. "Bon appetit," he said and left.

"This is just a guess, you understand, but I think DeMio doesn't know how to handle people like Ward Griswold or Nick Abbott."

"Could always shoot 'em," LaCroix said. "Works in Chicago."

I ignored his attempt at humor. "That bunch at Cherokee Point is just as secretive, just as isolated as the mob."

"Oh, Michael, get a grip," A.J. said.

"Seriously," I said. "They live in their own world, or try to, as much as the wise guys. Get involved with outsiders, get trouble." I don't think my fellow diners were impressed with my analysis. "How's the whitefish, ladies?" I said.

"Don't change the subject, Michael," LaCroix said. "I like my steak just fine, but you're stretching here, don't you think?"

"Yeah, I guess," I said, "but something about Cherokee Point bothered Carmine enough to warn his kid."

My phone chirped. I got it out and read the screen.

"Michael?"

"It's Fleener. They got Joey. Asking if I want to be there for questioning."

"When?" A.J. said.

"Tomorrow." I tapped out, "yes."

We finished our dinner and when the table was cleared, we ordered a Grand Pecan Ball to share. And coffee.

"Pretty tasty," Fran said. "Been a while since I've had one of these."

"And you live here?" A.J. said. "Shame on you." We laughed.

I sat back after a couple of bites of dessert and sipped my coffee. "Take a Cat off the Island at eight or nine," I said. "Get me to Petoskey in plenty of time."

"Oughta get interesting now," LaCroix said.

44

"**Y**ou asleep?" A.J. said, whispering.

"No. That noisy bunch of drunks. Can't get back to sleep."

"Me, either," A.J. said. We were lying on our backs in the dark, our legs and arms touching. The soft glow of a lamppost across the street came in the window and lit up the wall next to the bed. "Michael, I've been thinking . . ."

"About making mad, passionate love with me?"

"No."

"No?"

"Always like to think about making love to you, darling. Brightens my day. But, no, that's not on my mind right now."

"Aw."

"Oh, hush," A.J. said. "I was thinking about Parker Abbott, actually."

"We're on Mackinac Island, A.J., you know, *Lost in Time.*"

"That's *Somewhere in Time*, dear."

"Whatever."

"I'm serious, Michael," she said. "Listen for a minute."

"Okay," I said, "what?"

"In the office," she said. "With Sandy and Frank?"

"Yeah," I said. "Sheridan, too."

"Uh-huh. That time. When Sandy told you she was a survivor."

"I remember," I said, "all too well."

A.J. put her hand on my thigh, gently. "She thought Parker a likely survivor?"

"Yeah."

"Assume Parker is a survivor, for a minute," she said.

"Already done that, I guess," I said. "I trust Sandy. Wouldn't say something like that unless she believed it."

"Michael, that's your missing piece."

"What is?"

"Parker. Well, not Parker, herself," A.J. said. "Being a survivor."

"And?"

"Who told you something was missing in this case? Do you remember?"

I grabbed the extra pillow from the floor next to the bed and put it behind my head. I pushed myself up against the headboard. Really awake now.

"Pretty sure it was Fleener," I said.

"Okay, follow me here," A.J. said. "Cop in charge of the case thinks something's missing. You agree, right? Or at least you don't disagree."

I nodded.

"Everybody's first suspect is a family member. In this case, Nick. But he's got an alibi."

"Parker is not regarded seriously as a suspect," I said.

"On we go to the visiting hood from Chicago."

"Just like Carmine predicted."

A.J. propped her pillow up on the headboard and turned my way. "But the cops do nothing about Joey right away. Why not?"

"Parker and Joey alibi each other."

"Until Joey was arrested a few hours ago. Think an alibi has gone bye-bye?"

"Pretty smart for a newspaper editor," I said.

"It's the reporter side. More curious."

"Where does Parker being a survivor fit in?" I said.

"Every time a suspect comes up to bat, it's not Parker. Big coincidence, or she's one smart woman."

"I don't believe in coincidences," I said. "But is she capable of murder? Did she hate her father that much?"

"What did Kelsey Sheridan say? She hated her father and everyone knew it? For years?"

I nodded.

"Think Joey's lying? He lies to cover her and that gives him an alibi."

"Be a good thing for Fleener to keep in mind when he questions Joey tomorrow."

A.J. sat up and rearranged her pillows. "That's enough," she said. "Need some sleep. Cuddle up behind me."

"Okay," I said and moved in close. I put my arm over her shoulder.

"Feels good," she said.

45

"**W**hat time is it?" A.J. sounded like she had cotton in her mouth. "A little after six," I said, "go back to sleep."

"What are you doing?"

"Gonna run."

"Geez, Russo, get back in bed."

"Nah, I got time. Wanna run Crooked Tree, maybe Leslie. Can't do that at home."

"Shut up. Heard it all before." A.J. grabbed a pillow and plunked it over her head.

I laced up my Asics and pulled a gray, long-sleeved T from my bag. It said "Peace Frogs Mackinac Island" on the front. I put a room key in the pocket of my shorts and quietly closed the door behind me.

I went down the stairs and out the front door of the Windermere. The air was chilly and damp. The sun hid under a blanket of heavy clouds.

I stretched my calf muscles against a lamppost. And looked up and down Main Street for Santino Cicci. Didn't see him or anyone else. Maybe he and Rosato were out late last night.

I ran, slowly, up French Lane to Market Street, then right on Cadotte and started up the hill. The streets were almost empty. Two men in a golf cart moved along the fairway on the Grand Hotel course. By the time I got into the Annex, I was loose and running at a comfortable pace.

If A.J. was right. If Parker was smart enough to deflect attention. If Joey's alibi goes away. A lotta ifs, but there it is. Parker was a more serious suspect than I thought.

I crossed Garrison Road and went into the woods on Crooked Tree. A favorite stretch of packed dirt. Quiet, peaceful even, at the peak of tourist season. Seldom see anyone out here this early in the morning, but as I got close to Sugar Loaf, I spotted a figure about fifty yards up. I kept a steady pace. He wore black biking pants and jacket and a blue helmet. He stood in the road, holding a trail bike.

The man took off the helmet. It was Santino Cicci. He tucked the helmet under his left arm. When I was twenty feet away, he said, "Stop, Russo."

"No," I said, "training for a race." Ten feet away.

Cicci reached into his jacket pocket and pulled out a small Ruger automatic. "Stop."

I stopped. Five feet apart. "Don't like to mess with my training, Santino. Going to Arch Rock, out to the East Bluff and back downtown. Don't need a gun to follow me."

"Shut up, Russo," Cicci said. "LaCroix's not here this time. Just you and me."

"What ya gonna do, shoot me?"

"Don't tempt me, asshole."

"Oughta make DeMio real happy. Shooting me. You'd make the Chicago papers for that one. Think Carmine wants that?"

I slowly moved to my left, away from Cicci. I pointed down Sugar Loaf Road, towards Arch Rock. "Headed that way. Shoot me, but Carmine'll throw you off the coal dock if you do." With that I took off, a little faster than usual. Had I bluffed him? Nothing happened. I didn't look back. Not that crazy.

At Arch Rock, I took Huron to the top of the East Bluff and ran in front of the cottages lining the bluff. A fog had settled over the harbor. I usually like foggy, damp runs on the Island on days like this. No fun today. I looked up as I passed DeMio's house. If Cicci shot at me, Carmine could watch. No Carmine in the window. No gunshots either.

I took the stairs down to Main Street. People were out now, exercising or going to work. I relaxed with other people around. I ran straight through town, clicked my watch off at the hotel and walked out to the water on Windermere Point. No one followed. A long, dull-red ore boat, the *Edwin H. Gott,* moved slowly through the channel, riding low in the water.

It was still chilly and a light mist came down, but the run didn't feel as good as it should have. Of course, it's the first time a run has been interrupted by a man with a gun.

A.J. was sitting in the sunroom with a mug of coffee when I walked into the hotel lobby. I waved and went upstairs.

I'd finished my shower and was dressed in jeans and a sweatshirt when A.J. came into room. "Here's some coffee," she said. "Good run?"

"More or less," I said. "Thanks for the coffee." It tasted hot and strong. I decided not to mention Santino or his gun. For now, at least.

"We can make the eight o'clock if we hustle," A.J. said. "I paid the bill. Receipt's in your bag."

"All packed," I said and put down the empty cup. "I'll grab a Starbucks on the way."

Santino Cicci was not outside the hotel. I didn't see him on the way to the Arnold dock or in Starbucks, where I got coffee and a banana, or on the Catamaran. Could be he'd given up. More likely, he watched from somewhere else as the ferry left the harbor.

Our ride home was no faster than the trip up yesterday. We talked very little. We were too tired. Music from Interlochen Public Radio carried the day.

A.J. stopped in front of my building. "Got enough time?" she said.

"Yeah," I said and leaned over to kiss her. "Just have to change clothes."

"Call me later?" A.J. said.

"Yes."

"You gonna tell Hendricks or Fleener about Parker?"

"Probably."

46

"**A** bout time you got here," Hendricks said.

"Good morning to you, too," I said and looked at my watch. "I'm early." Martin Fleener sat in a chair by the glass. He held a plastic cup of coffee. "Marty," I said. He nodded.

Hendricks looked at me like I'd stumbled in off the street. "Nice of you to dress for the occasion," he said. I hadn't changed out of my jeans and sweatshirt.

"Who's that?" I said, nodding towards the man seated in the room on the other side of the glass. The man was in his fifties, not tall judging by how little of him showed above the table. His face was round and pink and his head was shaved clean. He wore a black pinstriped, double-breasted suit over a white spread collar shirt and a black and white striped tie.

"Who d'ya think it is?" Hendricks said.

"Joey's lawyer?"

"Of course it's Joey's lawyer." Hendricks said.

I looked at Fleener. "He get up on the wrong side of the bed?"

Fleener shrugged and said, "Phone calls came quick. Don got 'em."

"Who?"

"Started with a bang," Fleener said. "Senator Randall Harrison, representing the good people of Hoosier state, called all the way from the nation's capital."

Hendricks said, "Then Griswold called, Nick Abbott, Abbott's lawyer." He turned towards Fleener and me. "'Happy we got the real killer,' they said. 'Happy we're not bothering the Point anymore,' they said."

"If they're so happy, why are you so grumpy?"

"Because they're pushing, goddammit. Pushing to get Joey convicted and in prison. Like they pushed to keep us outta Cherokee Point in the first place." He turned back to the glass. "Those people are never satisfied. We never quite do it the right way. Goddamn good thing we got Joey. I'm tired of this."

"Yeah," Fleener said, "good thing." But Fleener's voice had a hollow ring to it. Would either of them want to hear about Parker?

The door to the interrogation room opened and in came Joey DeMio followed by a police officer. His lawyer stood up and they shook hands. DeMio was still in street clothes. Black jeans and a dark blue cotton jacket over a red V-neck sweater. The officer closed the door on his way out and Joey sat down.

"Who's the lawyer?" I said.

"Name's Otto Blatnic," Hendricks said, looking down at a yellow pad. "From Sterns, Blatnic in Chicago. Know him?"

"No," I said, "but Frank Marshall might." I pulled out my iPhone and tapped a message to Marshall.

"Ready, Marty?" Hendricks said.

"Whenever you say."

"Go."

Fleener got up, picked up a pad a yellow pad, a manila folder and his coffee. "Get more coffee first."

My phone chirped. I looked at the screen. "Wait up, Marty. It's Frank." Fleener stopped at the door. I read the screen. "Marshall doesn't know Blatnic, but the firm has a long rep as lawyers for the mob."

Fleener said, "Why am I not surprised?" He left the room and moments later sat down across the table from DeMio and Blatnic.

"For the record," Fleener said, "state your names."

For the next hour, Fleener asked mostly background questions, which Joey answered because Blatnic did not object.

"On the night of the murder," Fleener said, "where were you, Mr. DeMio?"

Blatnic's hand came from below the table and landed on DeMio's arm. His hand was as pink and chubby as his face.

"Don't worry counselor," Joey said. "Already told 'em where I was."

Blatnic looked at Fleener. "You already have this information, Captain. Move on."

I said to Hendricks, "Nice to have a suspect who tells his lawyer what to do."

Fleener opened the manila folder and shuffled through a page or two. "I believe you said you were with Ms. Parker Abbott. All night. Casino Motel." He looked up. "Do I have that right?"

"You don't have to answer that."

"I already did. More than once," Joey said, sounding bored.

"We have Ms. Abbott's statement that you were together all night."

"Good," Blatnic said. "Now move on."

"Don," I said, "anything wrong with Parker Abbott's alibi for Joey?"

"While you were gallivanting around the Island yesterday, we talked to Ms. Abbott."

"Here?" I said, pointing at the glass.

Hendricks shook his head. "My office. With her lawyer. Without her brother."

"She still alibi Joey?"

"Yeah," Hendricks said hesitantly.

"What?" I said. "Did she change her story?"

Hendricks shook his head. "Same story. Didn't catch any mistakes from the last time. But something about the way she repeated the story. Details were the same, but her body language, tone of voice. Something's different."

"Marty heard her, too?"

"Yeah."

"Same reaction?"

Hendricks nodded. "Just not sure about Joey anymore."

"Joey still alibi Parker?"

"Yep. Clear, sharp, detailed."

"Just not sure about Parker's story anymore?"

"Nope."

"Does it matter if Joey holds to his story?"

Hendricks shook his head. "Not right now. We could charge Joey and see what happens, I suppose," Hendricks said. "Might pressure him."

"Not so sure about that," I said, nodding at the glass. "His big city lawyer seems to rattle more easily than he does."

"Uh-huh," Hendricks said.

Fleener closed his file, picked up his yellow pad and left the room. A moment later, he opened the door. He stood and stretched like a man who just got out of bed. "Well, Don?"

"I dunno. Joey's story hasn't changed. It's Parker Abbott's alibi for Joey that worries me." Hendricks got out of his chair. He looked at Joey and his lawyer, still seated on the other side of the glass. Hendricks turned to Fleener and said, "Tell you what. Charge Joey with the murder of Carleton Abbott. See what shakes out."

Fleener said, "Might break Parker's story."

"Think you ought to break Joey's story instead," I said. Hendricks and Fleener both looked at me.

Hendricks said, "Why would we want to do that?"

"Because Parker Abbott killed her father."

47

"**M**y office," Hendricks said and walked out. Fleener followed Hendricks and I followed Fleener out the door and down the hallway. Hendricks went behind his desk. Fleener took his usual chair on the right wall. I sat across from Hendricks.

"You better have a good explanation, Russo," Hendricks said.

"You really think Parker shot her father, Michael?" Fleener said. "Hard thing to do. Killing somebody. But your father?"

I sat up straighter in my chair. Hoped it would help. "You already broke the ice." I glanced from Hendricks to Fleener and back. "Both of you are hesitant about Joey as the shooter, right?"

"Just charged the asshole with murder," Hendricks said.

"That was a tactic, Don. You know that. 'See what shakes out.' That's what you said."

"What d'ya think, Marty?" Hendricks said.

"Don't know, Don," Fleener said. "He's right. You're hoping something'll pop because of the murder charge."

Hendricks was quiet for a moment. I heard laughter somewhere outside the office. People were having fun.

"Okay, Russo, I'll humor you. Convince me." Hendricks came forward in his chair. He leaned his elbows on the desk. "Convince me Parker Abbott shot her old man."

"It's family first in a case like this," I said. "But Nick Abbott had a solid alibi, so you crossed him off the list. Instead of turning to the next family member, you went for Joey DeMio."

"Obvious choice," Fleener said.

"Of course, it's the obvious choice," I said. "Hell, Carmine DeMio said the same thing to me before you ever talked to Joey."

Hendricks rolled his eyes, gestured my way and said, "Your new best friend." I ignored the comment.

"Because Joey was such as obvious choice . . . I mean, look at him. Mob guy, from Chicago, of all places. Spends time up here because his father lives on the Island. His money feeds Nick Abbott's blackjack habit. Money that Nick is slow to pay back, I remind you. Joey's very public romance with Parker. And the list goes on. So you never seriously considered Parker as the killer."

At least they were listening. Hendricks could have ended this quickly. Maybe they're less certain about Joey than I thought.

"On top of that, you got the irritating prima donnas out at Cherokee Point. First they push you away. Then they push a quick hanging for Joey. All the while throwing their weight around. Calls from a U.S. Senator?"

"Didn't jump on Joey that fast," Hendricks said, "most of the rest is true. But . . ."

"But?" I said.

"What you have not done is tell me why," Hendricks said. "Why would Parker Abbott kill her father? Grant you, she had plenty of opportunity. But why, Russo?"

"Don, I need a little room here."

"What does that mean?"

"I want a couple of days."

"Jesus Christ, Russo," Hendricks said, raising his voice. He picked up a green and white striped ballpoint pen and threw it down, hard, on the desk.

"Don," I said, raising my voice, "you got me into this."

"Don't remind me."

"I didn't ask for this job, goddammit ..." I stopped. Didn't finish the sentence. I lowered my voice and looked at Fleener, then back at Hendricks. "But you guys were in trouble when this all started. When you asked, well, I wanted to help. Cut me some slack. A couple of days, that's all."

"You got anything to give us?" Fleener said. "Any reason why we should, Michael? Other than us wondering about Parker's story."

"The murder weapon," I said. "Found it?"

"No," Hendricks said.

"I don't know where it is either," I said, "but she got it at Cherokee Point."

"Evidence?"

"Talk to the residents. Find out who's missing a gun."

"We did that, Michael," Fleener said. "Nothing."

"Of course not," I said. "Think that bunch would admit a thing like that?"

"We thought of that," Fleener said.

"Were you aware that no one out there locks their doors? Even if they're gone for days at a time? Lot of handguns and long guns out there. Be easy to walk in an empty house. Pick one up."

"Pick out a house?" Hendricks said. "Excuse me, a cottage, and waltz right in. Choose a weapon and walk out. Just that easy?"

"That easy if you grew up on the Point. Know the men with guns and where they kept 'em. Which ones are locked up, which ones aren't. Who's out of the house for an hour, who's gone for a week. Easy if you know all that."

"Sure Parker knew all that stuff?" Fleener said.

"You know Kelsey Sheridan?"

"The Dartmouth guy?" Hendricks said. "What about him?"

"Grew up there, too. Knew where the guns were. All the kids knew," I said. "Just like they knew who had extra booze. Take a bottle that wouldn't be missed."

Don Hendricks rubbed his hands over his face. He looked at Martin Fleener.

"One day," I said. "Two tops."

"Marty?" Hendricks said.

Fleener stood up. He pulled back his suit coat and stuck his hands in his pants pockets. He gently rocked back and forth on his heels. "Joey's not going anywhere," he said.

"Forty-eight hours, Russo," Hendricks said. "Now get out of here."

48

"**M**ichael, I'd like you to meet Rita Del Amo." Sandy said.

I came around from behind my desk and reached out my hand. "Dr. Del Amo," I said, "happy to meet you."

"Thank you," she said. "Please call me Rita."

"I will. Won't you sit down?" I gestured at the client chair. I went back to my chair and sat down. Dr. Rita Del Amo was five-six and a trim seventy-one years old. Her collar length, salt and pepper hair was brushed behind the ears. She wore no make-up that I could tell and only a little lipstick. A soft red. She was professionally dressed in a light gray two-piece suit over a black blouse with a large bow tied at the neck.

"Would you like some coffee, Rita?" Sandy said. "Just made a fresh pot."

"I would," Del Amo said, "with a little sugar."

"Michael?"

I nodded. "Thank you for coming to the office today," I said to Del Amo.

"You're welcome," Del Amo said. "I was reluctant when Sandy first talked to me about it."

"What changed your mind?"

"Sandy did," Del Amo said. "I'm certainly sympathetic to your predicament, but talking about a woman I've never met, that makes me uncomfortable, both professionally and personally. Sandy convinced me that you would accept my boundaries for a discussion like this."

"That's true," I said. "I hope that your professional opinion will help me decide what to do."

Sandy came in with two mugs of coffee and put them on the desk. "Back in a minute," she said.

Del Amo picked up her mug and took a sip. "Very nice." She put the mug back on the desk. "As I understand it, you must decide if you should talk to the police about a woman you think committed a serious crime because she was sexually abused."

"Close enough," I said.

"How would you state your problem then," Del Amo said.

"I've already told the police I believe the woman committed the crime," I said. "My gut tells me that she did it, at least in part, because she was raped as a child. Probably over a period of years." I picked up my coffee and drank some. "Do I tell the police what I think? Do I have the right to say something like that based on my instincts but we have no proof?"

Sandy returned with her own coffee and sat down.

Del Amo looked at Sandy and smiled. "It was not difficult to figure out who Sandy was talking about. This is a small community. We don't have very many murders around here. That's a good thing."

"Does it make a difference that we're talking about the Abbott family?" I said.

"Not really," Del Amo said. "I'm guessing anyway."

"Educated guessing," I said.

"If you say so."

"I do say so," I said. "You've spent most of your career helping survivors of sexual abuse rebuild their lives. Sandy might not have the life she does were it not for you."

"Sandy's the one who did the hard work," Del Amo said.

"I understand the distinction, but you have lots of experience. Certainly there are common characteristics among survivors."

She nodded.

"In light of your experience, might a woman kill her father because he raped her as a child?"

"I can't determine that."

"Is it possible?"

"Anything's possible."

"Is it probable?"

"I can't determine that either."

"That's not very helpful, doctor," I said, slightly annoyed.

"Michael," Sandy said, picking up on my irritation.

"Don't get frustrated with me, Mr. Russo," Del Amo said, calmly. "You're asking me to answer a specific question I cannot answer."

I sat back in my chair. "I'm sorry," I said. "I didn't mean to . . . it's just that I have to decide what to do."

"Michael," Sandy said. I looked at her. "I have an idea."

"Go ahead," I said.

"Rita, you know what he wants. I know you have to be careful what you say. Michael knows that, too. What are you comfortable saying?"

Del Amo picked up her coffee, took a sip while she gave Sandy's question some thought.

"I understand your problem," she said. "Really, I do. In fact, I respect you for trying to figure this out before talking to the police about it. I'm not sure most people would do that."

I nodded.

"Here's what I am comfortable saying. There are some characteristics here consistent with victims. Sexual abuse of a child by a parent or other trusted person, if not dealt with in a determined way with professional help, could produce enough anger to lead to violence. It's not a certainty, but it is a possibility, especially if other factors fuel the anger, too."

The office was quiet. I heard a car horn in the parking lot outside.

"I appreciate that," I said. "Thank you."

"You're welcome," Del Amo said.

"I understand from Sandy that you recently retired."

"Yes," Del Amo said. "It was a difficult decision, but I made it. I haven't looked back."

"I wish you good luck," I said.

"To you, as well," she said.

I thanked Dr. Rita Del Amo for her time. After she left the office, I stood at the window in the outer office. A light rain came down, but it was warm. Lake Street was crowded with people, mostly tourists, in from the beach on a rainy day. Summer had arrived in Petoskey, no matter the temperature or the rain. People waiting for the light at Lake and Howard, were stacked three deep in each direction.

"What are you going to do, Michael?" Sandy said.

"I was thinking about a sandwich at Julienne Tomatoes. Wanna go?"

Sandy shook her head. "Gotta run out to Home Depot. Rather do it now than after work. I meant what about Parker Abbott?"

"I know," I said. I turned away from the window. "Do two things before you head out, will you please?"

"Sure."

"Call Julienne Tomatoes and order me a 'You Asked For It' to go."

"That the chicken salad on the cherry pecan bread?"

"Yep," I said. "And call Hendricks. Tell him I want to talk to him and Fleener. Soon as he can set it up."

"You've decided?"

I nodded. "Guess so."

49

Sandy left the office. I pulled on my yellow rain slicker, put on my green hat, the one with a white Michigan State block "S" above the brim, and went into the rain. I walked up Lake and turned up Howard. Amazingly, I didn't want to wait for the light at the corner. I jaywalked. Does anyone say jaywalk anymore? The rain was no more than a heavy mist, but I zipped the jacket to my neck anyway. I crossed Mitchell, with the help of the stoplight this time, passed Penny's and went into Julienne Tomatoes.

The charming restaurant up Howard Street has served me soup, sandwiches and more than a few pecan rolls for more than a decade. For a hundred years, the building's been several businesses, including a feed store and a meat market. Bought my first cup of coffee the week the restaurant opened. Today, lunch to go.

The rain disappeared into the clouds on my way back to the office. I would tell Hendricks and Fleener that Parker Abbott had a motive for killing her father. Couldn't prove it. Not likely she'd admit it. But there it was. They could tell me to go to hell. They could put it into the mix, see if they can use it.

I hung my jacket on the coat rack. I got a bottle of water from the refrigerator, unpacked my sandwich and sat down to eat it. If they thought the motive believable, even if only a little, we had only one choice. Break Joey's alibi about being with Parker. Leaves her without a cover for the night of the murder.

I was down to the last two bites of my sandwich when Sandy came in. She put down a large shopping bag and hung up her coat.

"How ya doin' investigator-man? Solved the puzzle yet?"

"Not sure I know the puzzle," I said.

"Seems clear to me," Sandy said.

I rolled up the sandwich papers and put them in the wastebasket. "Knew there was a reason I hired you."

"Thank you."

"You wanna tell me before Labor Day?"

"The puzzle?"

"Hurry up or I'll fire you," I said.

"How do you get Joey DeMio to admit he wasn't with Parker Abbott on the night of the murder?" Sandy said. "Plain enough for you?"

"Got any ideas how to do that?" I said.

"Solving the puzzle's your problem, boss. That's why you get paid the big bucks."

50

The rain had not come back when I left for Hendricks' office. The sidewalks were still thick with people— singles, couples, families, all convinced there was no point going to the beach this afternoon. The sidewalk emptied quickly once I passed the American Spoon Café. Not many tourists care about visiting the county offices. That's as it should be.

Hendricks got a fresh cup of coffee, but I passed. Fleener had a bottle of water.

Fleener looked as fresh as he always did, no matter the time of day. Jacket, tie and shirt all tidy and neat. Hendricks was rumpled. Coat on the hall tree in the back corner of his office, sleeves rolled up to the elbow and tie pulled away from his throat.

Hendricks drank coffee, then said, "Well, you didn't take as long as I thought you would."

I shrugged. "Things work out sometimes."

Hendricks leaned back in his chair, laced his fingers together, hands behind his head. He looked smug or annoyed. Couldn't tell which one. "So you think Parker Abbott killed her old man. That right?"

I nodded.

"Are you ready to tell us why," he said, nodding towards Fleener.

"Yes," I said, "I am."

"Then enlighten us, will you please." No wondering this time. Sarcasm, pure and simple.

"Like everyone else, once Nick Abbott's alibi checked out, I figured Joey was the guy. He made it simple for us, too. But every so often, a small monkey wrench got thrown into the mix. Gave me second thoughts."

I spent the next several minutes recapping the contributions of Kelsey Sheridan, Carmine DeMio, A.J. Lester and finally, Sandy Jeffries' thoughts about Parker Abbott.

"When you two guys said you had doubts about Joey, well, that put it all into play."

Fleener spoke first. "So you think the abuse of Parker . . . sorry, the possibility that she was abused by her father, was the piece I couldn't find?"

"Part of it," I said. "You had doubts about Joey, now you got another suspect, right?"

"Maybe," Fleener said. "Not convinced yet."

"Don't have to be convinced," I said, "just give it enough room to play out."

"Don?" Fleener said.

"It's a stretch is what I think," he said.

"About Parker?" I said.

"Yeah. Trouble is my doubts about Joey grow every time we talk about this case." Hendricks leaned forward, opened a manila folder on his desk and sifted through several sheets. "One minute, fuck it, Joey did it, let's move on. Next minute, well, too easy to pin it on Joey."

"So where does that leave you?" I said.

"Still a stretch, Russo, but . . ."

"Want to play it out, Don?" Fleener said.

Hendricks shook his head. "Not yet. Let's do it on paper first." He closed the folder. He looked at me, hard. "Start with DeMio, that's what you said?"

"Yeah. Gotta break his alibi for Parker."

"Got an idea about that?" Hendricks said.

"If Parker's support for Joey's gone soft, like you guys think, she's gonna dump the alibi. Only a matter of when."

"That's possible," Fleener said.

Hendricks nodded.

"Let's use that. Tell Joey Parker's bailed on her alibi and he's going away for murder," I said.

"Think Joey D., famous Chicago hood, is gonna buy a ploy like that?"

"Pretty cocky the last time you had him in the room. Thinks we're all hicks from West Bum-Fuck up here," I said. "Think you could play that to your advantage, Marty?"

"I could wear a better suit, different tie. Might help," Fleener said.

"You don't have any bad suits, Marty," Hendricks said.

"I'll fake it then," Fleener said. "Might be another way."

"That would be?" Hendricks said.

"Have the counselor, here," Fleener gestured my way, "talk to Joey. With his lawyer in the room, of course."

"Joey's lawyer'd object to that," Hendricks said. "Or Joey."

"And if one of them doesn't, Carmine will," I said. "No, this is better left to a pro."

"Your confidence in my skill is appreciated, but you comin' at him, not being a cop and all, might work better," Fleener said. He took a drink of water and put the bottle on the floor next to his chair. "You could make it more believable. Makes more sense to have Russo do it, Don."

"Don't like it," Hendricks said, "don't like amateurs doing our job. No offense, Michael, but Marty's experience counts for a lot."

"I'm with you, Don. Marty should do it, but I'll do it if you two think it's the best option."

"Either way," Hendricks said, "Gotta tell Otto Blatnic. Can't just put you in there without telling him first. You okay with that, Marty?"

Fleener said, "I am."

"Russo?"

"Me, too," I said.

"Then Mr. Otto Blatnic decides which one of you gentlemen gets to play his client."

51

Robin Savage sat in the client chair. We finished her divorce two days ago.

"I never thought it would go so well when we started," Savage said. "I was so screwed up after Steven walked out." She shook her head.

"You got a really good deal," I said. "Of course, it helped, as you pointed out, that your husband . . ."

"Ex-husband, I'm delighted to say."

"Right. That your ex-husband was more interested in his girlfriend than the details of the settlement. You probably could have gotten more."

Robin Savage shook her head. "Didn't want to gouge him. Though the son-of-a-bitch deserved it. Just wanted fair and wanted out."

My desk phone blinked twice. Sandy was on the other end.

"Excuse me, Robin," I said and picked up the receiver. "Yes?"

"Michael, sorry to interrupt," Sandy said. "Mr. Carmine DeMio is here to see you."

"Seriously?"

"Yes." She said with an even tone.

"Tell him have a seat, be with him in a moment."

"Not the smart option," Sandy said. "Especially considering the, ah, gentlemen with him."

"More than DeMio?"

"Uh-huh."

"Be right out." I hung up the phone. "Robin, I'm sorry but something has come up. Unexpectedly."

She picked up her purse from the floor and stood. "That's okay. We're done anyway," she said. "Hah. We are done, all done, aren't we?"

"Yes, we are," I came around the desk and we hugged briefly. I opened the door to the outer office and Robin Savage walked by me.

"Thanks, again, Michael," she said and left.

"Mr. DeMio," I said. "Welcome to my office." DeMio had dressed well for a business meeting. Gray sharkskin, single-breasted suit, black shirt and a black and gray striped tie. Natty for Chicago, I guess. "Would you like to come in?"

DeMio started for my office and so did the men with him. Gino Rosato, looking sloppy and overweight as always. The traveling barrister from Chicago, Otto Blatnic. And Mr. Santino Cicci, wearing bruises on his left cheek, his forehead and his chin. A wide bandage covered the bridge of his swollen nose. Looked broken.

"Not you, gentlemen." I said. "Just Mr. DeMio."

DeMio stopped and turned. He looked at me. "I want Blatnic."

I nodded.

"Gino, Santino. Sit." Rosato made for a chair, but Cicci glared at me.

"What happened, Santino? Little kid knock ya off your bicycle?"

He took one step in my direction.

"Santino," DeMio said. "Sit." And Cicci joined Rosato on the other side of the front office.

"Had to shave your goatee because of the cut?" I said.

DeMio said, "Don't push your luck, counselor. Let's go." Blatnic followed DeMio. I closed the door behind us. I took my chair. DeMio sat across from me, Blatnic on the left wall.

"What can I do for you?" I said.

"Mr. Blatnic, here, tells me you want to talk to my son. While he's in custody. That right?"

"Only if I have to."

"What does that mean?"

"It means that if Don Hendricks and Mr. Blatnic agree, I'll talk to Joey, with Mr. Blatnic in the room. Instead of Captain Fleener."

"Why would you do that?" DeMio said.

"Joey's innocent."

"Hell, I know that." DeMio said.

"He didn't kill Carleton Abbott."

"You can prove it?"

"No."

"No?" DeMio said sharply.

"Not yet, anyway."

"What does that mean?"

"It means, not yet I can't."

DeMio was quiet. Couldn't tell if he was thinking or about to leave.

"Why did you come to the mainland?" I said.

"Bail hearing," he said. "Only second time off the Island since April."

"What was the other time?"

"What?"

"Said this was your second trip. Why'd you leave the Island the first time?"

"You're pissing me off, Russo," he said. The strain showed in his face.

"Don't care," I said.

"People don't talk to me that way, counselor."

"Don't care about that, either," I said. "Look, you barge in here without an appointment. You bring," I gestured towards the front office, "Laurel and Hardy out there. Get pissed when I tell you I can help Joey. Why should I be nice?"

DeMio didn't say anything.

"I'll say it again. I don't think Joey killed Carleton Abbott. Can't prove it just yet, but the cops are listening to me. And you're pissed? 'Bout time you went back to the East Bluff."

He was quiet, then said, "Who killed Abbott?"

I shook my head. "Between me and the cops."

"But you want to talk with Joey?"

"Me or Fleener," I said. "With Blantic there."

DeMio eased back in the chair. "Not you," he said. "If my boy gets questioned, gotta be official." He looked at Blatnic. "Got that?" Blatnic nodded. "You got that, counselor?" I nodded.

He stood, so did Blatnic. DeMio arranged his suit coat, buttoned it and turned for the door. Rosato and Cicci got up when their boss came into the room. He went for the door with Blatnic close behind.

"Wear a helmet next time, Santino," I said.

He ignored me. Cicci and Rosato followed DeMio down the stairs.

I went to the front window. Sandy followed.

"Scary guys," she said.

"Yes, they are."

The four men appeared on the sidewalk below our window. They turned right.

"Maybe they're going to the bookstore," Sandy said sarcastically. "What's he doing?" she said, pointing at Cicci, who'd stopped to stare across Lake Street. My eyes moved. Leaning on a parked car was Henri LaCroix. He waved at Cicci and smiled broadly.

"See Henri?"

"Yep."

Santino Cicci turned and caught up to the others.

"Wonder what that was about," Sandy said.

"Let's ask him," I said. LaCroix crossed the street and climbed the stairs.

Our door was still open. Sandy and I waited.

Henri LaCroix came through the door. "Sandy. Michael. Good to see you. Been too long." He wore jeans, black, a white polo shirt and a light tan jacket. Covers a gun on a warm day.

Before I could get a word out, Sandy said, "What was that all about?"

"Outside?"

"Uh-huh," she said.

"With Santino?"

"Yes, Santino," Sandy said. "Don't play cute."

"You just happened to be in downtown Petoskey," I said, "for Carmine DeMio's second trip off the Island this season."

LaCroix held up his right hand. Four fingers. "Fourth time, but he doesn't talk about that."

"He lied about trips off the island?"

LaCroix nodded. "Gets himself all messed up. Ripped jeans, dirty T-shirt, torn running shoes, hat pulled down. Goes to the casino. St. Ignace and the Sault."

"Gambler?"

LaCroix shook his head. "Spends a few bucks. Watches the operation."

"The Indian casinos are his?" I said.

"No. Wants to learn. See what they're doing, how they do it. Wants to make his places better, smoother, more cost efficient."

We sat down. Sandy at her desk, LaCroix and I in the client chairs recently occupied by our visitors.

"Whatever turns you on," Sandy said. "But what was that little dance with Santino Cicci? He glared at Michael, too. Up here."

"Got a burr up his ass about something," LaCroix said.

"You have anything to do with his black eye and bruises?"

"Me?"

"It was you, wasn't it?" I said. "Why'd you beat him up?"

"Just roughed him up some," he said. "Told him to leave you two alone," LaCroix said. "Didn't listen. That little stunt at Sugar Loaf, when you were running? Had to teach him a lesson."

"Didn't need to do that, Henri," I said. "I handled the situation all right."

"Not about you. I warned him off. Now he knows I meant what I said."

"Henri's rules?"

Henri smiled. "By the way, Michael, you were lucky. This time. Better learn to take care of yourself. Just a friendly word of advice."

LaCroix looked at his watch. "Oops. Gotta go. Want to catch the four-thirty ferry. Meeting Fran for a hamburger at Seabiscuit at five." He got up and walked away. "See you next time, kids."

Sandy shook her head.

"What?" I said.

"Not so long ago, Robin Savage was our typical client. That's when you were a lawyer."

"Still a lawyer."

"Yeah? Tell it to the guys who just left," Sandy said.

"Could be good at it."

"I know."

"I like the work," I said. "You okay with that?"

She nodded slowly. "Just not used to it yet," she said.

"Me either. But might do more of it."

"Then Henri's right. You need to get better at protecting yourself. Do something. There'll always be another Santino Cicci."

I nodded. "Afraid you're right," I said.

"Where do we go from here?" Sandy said.

"Time to lay it out for Hendricks."

"About Parker Abbott?"

I nodded. "And get Joey to drop his alibi for her." I got up. "Got time for a run," I said. "Meeting A.J. at Chandler's after she's done with work."

"Good luck with Hendricks," Sandy said.

52

"That felt nice," A.J. said. She put her head on my chest and pushed up tight against the side of my legs. "Have I told you lately that I love you?"

"This morning,"

"This morning?"

"Uh-huh."

"We didn't sleep together last night. You were home."

"Sent me a text when you got to work," I said. "With one of those funny faces blowing a kiss."

A.J. laughed and kissed my chest. "Forgot," she said. "Sometimes I think we're too busy. It's lousy when things are so complicated I can't remember a love note to you."

"Shouldn't last much longer," I said. "You're still making progress on the e-edition, right?"

"Yeah. We've made the pages less confusing. People get the stories they want to read with fewer clicks. It's going pretty well, I'm happy to say." A.J. kissed my chest again. "Such a nice evening. Once I got to Chandler's. Sorry I was so late."

"Didn't mind waiting," I said. "It gave me a chance to let go of the Abbott thing before you got there. The extra glass of wine wasn't bad either."

"You looked yummy when I saw you in that navy blazer," she said. "Wanted to jump your bones right there."

"Glad you waited," I said. "Needed to nibble on some food before I nibbled on you."

"Worth the wait," she said. "Hope things ease up for you, too. Still plan to tell Hendricks what you think about Parker?"

"Meeting him in the morning. Fleener, too."

"You still okay saying Parker Abbott was sexually abused?"

"Yes. No. Just don't know," I said.

"Maybe it's the reporter in me, but I'd want to have more than one source confirm an accusation like that before I'd write the story."

"I'm not accusing Parker of anything," I said. "Quite the contrary. Her father's the one who should be accused."

"Didn't mean it that way, sorry." A.J. lifted her head off my chest and rose up on one elbow. "Bringing sex abuse into this case is, I dunno, it's hard. Changes things."

"It is hard," I said. "But Hendricks expects me to lay out a motive. I'll do the best I can. He'll decide to use it or not."

"Still convinced it's the best way to go?"

"As much as I can be about anything in this case."

53

Don Hendricks leaned back in his chair. "I don't know, Russo. Lotta guesswork."

"It's better than guesswork, Don," I said.

"Not much."

"The pieces add up. Assuming Parker Abbott was sexually abused by her father explains a lot. The anger, for one thing."

"Could be part of the motive, Don," Fleener said. "The man treated every woman like dirt, remember? Even his daughter. Nick got it all. The money, the power, his father's nasty streak."

Hendricks nodded. "Maybe."

"We're nowhere unless Joey changes his story," Fleener said. He looked at his watch. "He'll be here in a minute. What do you want to do?"

Hendricks took a deep breath and said to Fleener, "If Joey backs away from the alibi for Parker, we'll see. First things first."

Otto Blatnic waited patiently at the table on the other side of the glass. His pudgy hands played nervously with a ballpoint pen.

The door opened and an officer brought in Joey DeMio. He wore jailhouse orange. The officer closed the door when he left and Joey sat next to Blatnic.

"Time to go to work," Fleener said, picking up two manila folders.

"Marty," I said, "remember to ask him how many times Parker visited him."

"She hasn't been here at all," Hendricks said.

"I know," I said. "Ask how many times. And ask if he's seen her since Abbott was killed."

Fleener went into the room, took off his black, double-breasted blazer and carefully hung it over the back of his chair. He placed the two folders on the table, opened the top one and finally sat down.

"Gentlemen, for the record . . ."

"Maybe Joey'll get annoyed. Like last time," Hendricks said. "Try to tell Otto, there, how it should go."

"We should be so lucky," I said.

"More Fleener than luck this time," Hendricks said. "He'll get him pissed in a little while."

Fleener worked well-worn ground, again and again. Blatnic kept telling Fleener to "move on," but he diplomatically ignored him. Blatnic tried to keep Joey under control, but mostly gave up after Joey proclaimed "told 'em already" one too many times. Maybe he decided to wait for new questions or new territory.

"Well, Joey," Fleener said. "How's your girlfriend doing?"

"Which one?" Joey said and laughed.

Fleener smiled liked he got the joke. "Well, Joey, I suppose we could start with the 'As' and work our way through all of 'em. What d'ya say?"

"Sure, why not," Joey said. "Start with 'A' for piece of Ass." He laughed hard at that one.

Fleener chuckled approvingly.

"Joey, please," Blatnic said.

Joey waved his hand at Blatnic dismissively.

"How about 'A' for Abbott, Joey D.," Fleener said, sharply. "Let's start with her."

"Parker Abbott?"

"Uh-huh."

"Miss rich-and-famous?" he said with a grin. He glanced at Blatnic, then leaned forward, like he was about to share a secret. "Great piece of ass," he said, still grinning. "Woman knows how to give head, let me tell you."

"So I've heard," Fleener said.

"Hear we go," Hendricks said.

"What?" Joey said to Fleener. "What d'ya mean?" His smugness vanished.

"Come on, Joey D. Guys talk, you know that."

"About Parker?"

Fleener nodded. "Woman gives a great blow job. Man's gonna hear about it."

"Cops?"

"Cops, sure, civilians, too," Fleener said.

I said to Hendricks, "I'm surprised Joey took the bait."

"Joey's over confident, Russo," Hendricks said. "Got power to make tons of money, even kill people. Thinks he's smarter than his lawyer, smarter than a cop. Tough as nails until you catch 'em off guard."

"Hey, Joey D.," Fleener said. "Think you're the only guy she bops?"

Hendricks said, "Look at Joey. Doesn't know what to do. Marty knocked him off his game. He'll needle him a while longer."

Fleener toyed with Joey, moving rapidly from the night of the murder, to women, to Parker and back again. Blatnic interrupted here and there, but Joey paid little attention. Then . . .

"Abbott come and see you in jail?" Fleener said.

"Huh?"

"You heard me. Has Parker Abbott come to see you?"

"Yeah," Joey said, waving his arm like, "of course."

"Really?" Fleener opened the other manila folder. "Not what it says here," he said, picking up a sheet paper. "Says here you had only two visitors. Your father, once, and Mr. Blatnic, here."

"But . . ."

"No buts about it, Joey D." Fleener said. "The woman dumped you. Probably in London or Rome right now. Bopping some new guy."

Joey sat back in his chair. He looked as if he'd been slapped.

"In fact, Joey D., how many times you seen her since the night you killed her father?"

"No," Blatnic said, loud and sharp. His pudgy hand landed on Joey's forearm like a mallet. "Don't answer that. You know better than that Captain. What are you trying to pull?"

Fleener shrugged. "Okay. How many times you seen her since the night of the murder?"

"Well," Joey said, "ah, you know . . ."

"How many, Joey D?" Fleener said. "The woman who slept with you the night her father was killed? You can't remember? The woman who gives great head and you can't remember?"

"Sure, I can," Joey said without conviction.

"Joey," Fleener said. "Were you with Parker Abbott the night of the murder?"

"Don't answer that." Blatnic roared. "Next question."

"Joey. Are you covering for Parker Abbott?"

"Don't answer that," Blatnic said. "Not a word."

Joey kept quiet.

"Where're you going with this Captain?"

Fleener ignored him. "Are you covering for her?"

"Don't answer that," Blatnic said again. "Tell me what you're up to or this stops now."

"Joey, were you with Parker Abbott the night of the murder?"

"No," Blatnic said. "No more of this."

"Were you, Joey?"

"Yeah, I was with her," Joey said. He looked dazed. "Of course I was."

"Know what I think?" Fleener said. "I think Parker Abbott killed her father. You weren't with her at all. That's what I think."

"What?" Joey said.

Blatnic didn't move.

"I think Parker Abbott killed her father and suckered you to cover for her."

"No," Joey said weakly.

"Yes, Joey D. You're covering for her. You got suckered, my man."

Joey shook his head, like he was trying to make a point.

"There it is, Joey D.," Fleener said. "You gave her an alibi, now it's your ass in a wringer. Feel good to be a sucker?"

"It wasn't like that," Joey said. "We were at the casino. Like I said."

"Bullshit," Fleener said. "She shot him and you're going down for it."

"Not like that," Joey said, shaking his head.

"Just like that, Joey D." Fleener sat back and closed both files. "Go ahead, Joey D., pull a Whitey Bolger. Don't be a rat. Be a stand-up guy. Know where that'll get you? Prison, my man. That's where it'll get you."

Joey sat back in the chair, arms loosely folded in his lap. Blatnic leaned over, close to his ear. He said something. Joey's head moved. It wasn't a nod. Blatnic said something more.

"Go ahead," Blatnic said to Joey.

Joey DeMio sat up straight, but didn't lean forward. He looked at Fleener.

"Joey, were you with Parker Abbott night of the murder?"

Blatnic let the question go this time.

Joey slowly shook his head. "No," he said. "No. Don't know where she was."

"A few minutes with my client," Blatnic said.

Hendricks tapped on the glass. Fleener got off the chair, took his coat and left the room. He came through the door a moment later.

"Don't that beat all," Fleener said.

"Sure does," Hendricks said. "Good job, Marty."

"Thanks."

Blatnic and DeMio huddled together, hands over their mouths. Blatnic did most of the talking, judging by how much his hands moved. We couldn't hear them.

"What about Parker Abbott?" I said.

Hendricks looked at Fleener and said, "Pick her up."

54

Frank Marshall put down a paper bag. I got two coffees. We sat at a small two-top in the window at Johan's Bakery, across Spring Street from the hospital. Traffic was thick.

"The two chocolate donuts are mine," he said. "Plain ones are yours."

I took out a donut and bit off a sizable chunk. "Ah, donuts and coffee. Must have been a cop in another life."

Marshall laughed. "I'd say you're doing your chosen profession proud."

"You mean as a lawyer or an investigator?"

"Lawyer," he said. "Clear a man of murder charges is something to be proud of."

"Thanks," I said, "but Martin Fleener did the hard work."

"I know," Marshall said, "but you helped put those two men in the room together, Michael."

I nodded and drank some coffee. "Didn't take Marty very long," I said. "Seemed like he got DeMio to drop his story pretty easily."

Marshall was on his second chocolate donut already. "Just looked that way. It wasn't easy at all." He drank some coffee.

"You ever watched him work?" I said.

"Once. Several years ago. Client of mine got caught in a terrible jam. I got him a criminal attorney." Marshall licked chocolate off a finger and drank more coffee. "Watched from the other side of the glass. My guy was okay in the end. Gave me a chance to watch Fleener." Marshall took a fresh napkin from the holder. "You watched any other cops, Michael?"

"A few times in Detroit," I said. "Another lifetime ago. I'd tag along sometimes when the firm represented a bad guy."

"Well, Martin Fleener plays at a different level when he needs to. Like LeBron James." Marshall shook his head. "The game looks familiar, but . . ."

"Want more coffee?" I said.

"Please."

I went to the counter to fill our cups.

"I knew a few cops like Fleener in Chicago," he said. "Ask them how they do it, they'd shrug and give some vague answer about experience."

"But experience is part of it?"

Marshall nodded. "Sure. Gotta learn how to handle yourself. Recognize bullshit. That stuff." Marshall looked in the bag hoping a third donut had materialized. It hadn't. "If you can pin one of 'em down. Get him to be honest. It's instinct more than anything else. They can't explain it. They just know which way to go."

"Rookies can't do that?" I said.

"Of course not," Marshall said. "Experience is the foundation. But trusting your instincts when your head tells you otherwise? You got it or you don't. Fleener's got it. Most don't."

"You miss working, Frank?"

Marshall looked out the window. Maybe the question took him to another place. He turned his head my way. "When I talk about some aspect of the job, yes, I miss it. Most of the time I don't. I had a good run. Don't want to work that hard anymore."

"You've been a big help to me," I said.

"Thanks. I've enjoyed it. Like dusting off the cobwebs. It's been fun."

"Maybe you could teach an evening course, 'How to be a Trained Investigator' in ten weeks."

"One student's enough," he said, pointing his index finger straight towards me. "Sometimes you don't listen to the teacher."

I shrugged.

"Have they brought Abbott in yet?"

"Don't know," I said. "Hendricks told her yesterday to come in with a lawyer."

"When do you go over for the interview?" he said.

"After lunch."

Marshall moved his empty cup aside and crumpled up the bag. "Does Parker Abbott know that Joey ratted her out?"

I shook my head. "Bet Fleener will use that bit of information to his advantage."

"Count on it."

55

"Find out about her lawyer?" Don Hendricks said. I sat with Hendricks and Marty Fleener. The room on the other side of the glass was empty, but Parker Abbott and her lawyer were on their way.

"I talked with Bill Stapleton after you called. Remember Stapleton?"

"Your friend with the fancy sports cars?" Fleener said.

"Yeah. His firm's represented Cherokee Point Resort Association for years. First place they'd go for a lawyer."

"What'd he have to say?" Hendricks said.

I took a small notebook from my brief bag and opened it. "Susan Klein is a partner at Pennington, Gray and Stapleton. Been there twelve years. Cal Berkeley Law. Lives in Bloomfield Hills with her husband and two children. Husband's at Ford Motor. She's fifty-four years old. Most important for you guys, Klein's a respected criminal attorney. Billy likes her personally and professionally. Says she's smart, quick and tough."

"Be who I'd call if I shot somebody," Fleener said.

"You can't afford her," Hendricks said.

"Story of my life," Fleener said with a laugh.

"Did your friend say if Klein's on retainer for Cherokee Point?" Hendricks said.

"On retainer? Folks at Cherokee Point, criminals?" I said sarcastically.

"Smart-ass," Fleener said.

"Thank you."

"So what did he say?"

"Not on retainer," I said. "Ward Griswold called for . . ."

"Griswold?" Hendricks said, turning my way. "Why'd he call to get Parker Abbott a lawyer?"

"It's all about the Point, remember? How it's gonna look? What'll people say?"

"Center of the fucking universe," Fleener said.

"Something like that."

"All right," Hendricks said with a sigh. "Anything else we should know?"

"That's it," I said, "but if Billy likes her, that's good enough for me."

There was a knock at the door. It opened and an officer leaned in. "They're here," she said.

"Thank you," Hendricks said.

"I'll wait outside, sir."

"Officer?"

"Sir?"

"Whatever happens in there, don't go in."

"But, sir, I . . ."

"Officer. We clear?"

"Yes, sir." And she closed the door behind her.

Parker Abbott walked in the room, followed by a woman we took to be Susan Klein. She was five-two, about 130, with a round shape. Her face was round, tanned, and her black hair had short streaks of gray at the temples. She wore stylish, rectangular glasses with deep red frames. She carried a black Coach brief case which went nicely with her tailored black suit.

Parker wore faded jeans and a lavender cotton crewneck sweater. She carried a bottle of water.

The two women sat at the table. Parker leaned on her elbows. She looked bored, annoyed. Klein put her hand on Parker's arm. Abbott pulled both arms off the table. Klein shot her a quick look.

"Not a good sign," I said.

"For them," Hendricks said. "Ready Marty?"

"Guess so."

"You got a plan?" I said.

"Ease into it, throw something out, see what happens."

"That's your plan?"

"One I got," he said. Fleener got out of his chair and picked up three manila folders.

"Good luck," Hendricks and I said, almost at the same time.

Fleener walked into the room, introduced himself to Susan Klein, said hello to Parker. He took off his suit jacket and put it on the back of his chair. He opened one of the files and sat down.

"For the record . . ." Fleener worked through a few basic sets of questions about Parker's life, family, Cherokee Point, life in Northern Michigan. Parker answered the questions, but was clearly unhappy with being in the chair and being questioned.

"Am I under arrest?" she said suddenly.

Before Fleener could answer, Klein jumped in, "No, Parker," she said, "you're not under arrest."

"Then I want to leave." She started to get up, but Klein grabbed her forearm.

"Sit down, Parker," she said. "Please."

"We have to clear up some loose ends," Fleener said.

"Thought we'd done that," Parker said.

"Please, Parker," Klein said, "sit back down. Answer the questions and that'll be it." Parker dropped herself in the seat, quite put out at the whole idea.

"Not a happy woman," I said.

Hendricks shook his head. "Nope."

"What loose ends?" Parker said.

"Where were you on the night your father was killed?"

"I've been through it already," she said.

Klein said, "Parker, we'll be out of here faster if you answer the questions."

Parker nodded. "With Joey DeMio."

"All night?"

Parker nodded.

Fleener covered the night of the murder, emphasizing details. Parker answered the questions, annoyed at having to go over it again.

"Joey DeMio's a pretty good guy? Nice man?"

"Sure."

"Treat you nice, buy you nice things, take you nice places?"

"I buy what I want. Don't need him for that."

"Sure, but Joey's dangerous, right? A tough guy from Chicago, if you know what I mean. Exciting. On the edge. Right?"

"If you say so," Parker said.

"Well, what then, just another dick in your bed?"

"Captain," Klein said, sharply. "Not appropriate."

Parker laughed.

"Doesn't matter," Fleener said. "Joey's got lots of women."

Parker didn't laugh.

Fleener opened another folder. "Let's see," he said. "Carleton Abbott. Quite a man, your father. Successful manufacturing business. Owns three patents for a particular process he developed. Long history at Cherokee Point. Part of the founding generation, or whatever it's called. Loving father to your brother and you . . ."

"I'm well acquainted with my father, Captain," Parker said. "I do not need you to tell me what I already know."

Fleener ignored her. "Says here he worked tirelessly for Catholic charities in Lake Forest and Chicago. Won several awards from the church. 'Outstanding Citizen' for 2003. Says here he was 'most beloved' by the congregation. What a guy. Can't imagine why anyone would kill him, can you? A really good guy, your father."

Parker sat with her arms folded across her chest.

"What d'ya think, Parker? Why'd anybody kill him?"

"Beats me," she said. "You're the cop. You tell me."

"I see two good men, men who've treated you like a princess. Pretty lucky woman, Parker."

No response.

"Where were you on the night your father was shot?"

"She answered that already," Klein said.

"Well, counselor, I'd like to hear it one more time."

"Go ahead," Klein said, "tell him."

"I was with Joey DeMio," she said. "Why don't you ask him, instead of me."

"Here it comes," Hendricks said.

"I did," Fleener said. "He said you weren't with him. Said he didn't see you that night."

Parker Abbott sat up, ramrod straight, her eyes as round as small saucers. "That son of a bitch," she said. "He lied."

"That nice man, man who bought you stuff. Couldn't be that mean?"

"Hell he couldn't."

Klein said, "Captain, has Mr. DeMio retracted his statement about him and Parker on the night of the murder?"

"Yeah," Fleener said, looking at Parker. "Joey retracted his story. Didn't know where you were that night. Didn't care, either."

Parker was angry and getting angrier. She muttered something under her breath.

"What was that, Parker?" Fleener said.

Parker shook her head.

"Joey said you used sex to sucker him into an alibi. Made him do it. That what happened, Parker, you sucker Joey into the alibi? After all the good times?"

"Bullshit," she said. "He's just like all the rest, the son of a bitch. Can't trust 'em. Can't believe a word they say."

"They, who?"

"Who?" Parker said. "Who the fuck do you think? Men, you asshole."

"Parker," Klein said, putting her hand on Parker's forearm again. Parker jerked her arm away.

"Men?" Fleener said. "I don't get it. You mean Joey? The guy who treated you well? That who you mean?"

Parker glared at Fleener.

"Not Joey?" he said. "Who then? Your father? The church loved him. You said he was a great father. Him?"

Parker was frozen in place. She said nothing.

"I don't get it, Parker," Fleener said. "Just don't get it. First you say Joey and your father are the best men on the planet, next thing you know, Joey's a son of bitch. Damn good thing your father's not like all the rest."

Parker didn't move.

"That's right, isn't it, Parker? Successful in business, beloved by his church, an icon of Cherokee Point. Your father . . ."

Parker Abbott exploded out of her chair. She lunged half way across the table towards Fleener. She slammed her fists down on the table, arms straight.

"Shut up, you son of a bitch, shut the fuck up. I've listened to bullshit about him all my life. My dad this, my dad that. Enough. I was nothing to him. He could have stopped it. Never did. He was never home. Didn't care what happened when I was a kid. Doesn't care now. I gotta go to a hospital, he said. Gotta get a shrink. Gotta get over it. I don't want a shrink. I want my money. It's my money, too." She was almost yelling.

"He was trying to help you?" Fleener said.

"He was trying to shut me up. Send me away. I was going to tell everyone what happened if he didn't leave me the fuck alone."

"Did your father rape you?"

"Stop," Klein said and grabbed Parker's arm, but she pushed it away. "Captain."

Fleener ignored her. "You were gonna tell people he attacked you?"

"What?"

"Your father attacked . . ."

Parker slammed her fists down on the table again. "It was my brother, you asshole, my brother. Shoved his cock in my mouth, that's what he did. I was twelve, thirteen. What difference does it make?"

Parker's face was red. Klein didn't move.

"The cock was the easy part," Parker said. "Didn't hurt. When he fucked me, it hurt. Goddamn, did it hurt. I'd bleed. My father didn't care.

Didn't stop it. My mother didn't care either, she . . . she'd yell at me. She had to wash the bloody sheets. My fault, she said."

The rigidity in her body slowly faded. Parker sat down. Her face was ashen, withered. Like she'd aged twenty years.

Her rage fell off, slowly, into tears. She cried quietly, like the shouting never happened "I was just a kid. It hurt so much. I was so scared. I prayed every night I wouldn't go to sleep. I wanted to hear Nick coming down the hall. I was so scared. If I didn't go to sleep, I'd hear him. My father never stopped it. Never tried. The son-of-a-bitch. The floors would creak. I could hear Nick coming."

She sobbed steadily now. She looked at Klein, then at Fleener. "I shot the son of bitch," she said. "I killed my father. He was gonna hide me in a hospital. Nick'd get everything. Why didn't . . ."

"That's enough," Klein said. "Not one more word."

"I was just a little kid. So scared. No place to hide."

No one moved. Or said anything. Just the hum of the air conditioning.

"A word with my client," Klein said, looking over Fleener's shoulder at the glass.

Hendricks rapped his knuckles on the glass. Fleener closed his folders, stood up and took his jacket off the chair. He came in with us. Fleener crossed his arms and we all looked at Parker Abbott. She was still crying. Klein held her in her arms.

"Good work, Marty," Hendricks said.

"Some days, I hate my job," Fleener said.

"Go home, Marty."

"I got reports . . ."

"Go home, Marty," Hendricks said. "Go home. Hug Helen. Have a drink. Reports'll wait 'till tomorrow."

"Okay."

We watched through the glass. Parker Abbott sat in the chair, still crying. There was nothing more to say.

56

"**W**hat'll happen to Parker Abbott?" A.J. said.

"Don't know," I said. "Up to Hendricks. He'll talk with Parker's lawyer, I'm sure."

I sat with A.J. and Henri LaCroix at a four-top on the deck at Mary's Bistro, next to the Star Line ferry dock. It was a very warm summer day. Fortunately, the sun had moved over the roof of the building, so we enjoyed the shade. Shepler's ferry, followed by one from Star Line, rounded the west breakwater and slowed down to reduce the wake in the marina.

A.J. sipped a Chardonnay. LaCroix drank a draft and chewed on pretzels. I had a Tanqueray gin and tonic.

"Did Hendricks have any reaction after Fleener finished the interview?"

"You asking as a reporter or as the love of my life?"

"Off the record," A.J. said.

I nodded. "Said he might have shot Abbott, too." I looked out, over the water. A long freighter, in need of fresh paint and weighed down with a hull full of cargo, moved slowly through the channel. The line of passengers on the Star Line dock waited patiently in the hot sun to board the ferry for Mackinaw City.

"Be nice if that'd help her," LaCroix said.

"It won't," I said. "But Hendricks and her lawyer'll get together, so who knows."

"What happened that night?" A.J. asked.

"Night Abbott was killed?" I said.

A.J. nodded.

"According to Parker, Carleton confronted her about going to the hospital for psychiatric help. She told him Nick's the one who needed a shrink, not her. When Abbott ignored that idea, Parker threatened to tell everyone still at the party about her father and her brother."

"Those people are something else," A.J. said.

"When Parker ran from the house, Abbott followed. Ended up at the tennis court."

"Where'd she get the gun?" LaCroix said.

"Hidden in her dresser. Underwear drawer." I shook my head.

"Why didn't the cops find the gun?" A.J. said.

"She put it back."

"What d'ya mean, she put it back?" LaCroix said.

"Parker stole it from one of the cottages. Guy's not there much. Never locks his door. She knew where the guns were."

"How long'd she have it?"

"Didn't remember when she took it, but she put it back soon after the shooting. No missing guns on the Point by the time anyone checked."

"Amazing," A.J. said. "So simple only an amateur would think of it."

"Those Cherokee Point guys made it tougher to find the gun, too."

"How so?"

"Believe they got a god-given right to their guns. Some are registered, some not. They didn't tell the cops about the unregistered ones."

"Before I forget," A.J. said, "what did Sheridan have to say when you told him?"

"That Kelsey Sheridan? From Cherokee Point?" LaCroix said.

"That's him," I said. "The would-be novelist. Revenge and hate. He had Parker pegged from the start. Of course father wasn't the rapist. She killed him because he didn't protect her from her sadistic brother and then tried to hide her away while Nick got everything."

"And nobody believed him," A.J. said.

"Including me," I said. "He was surprised when I told him his fictional plot was closer to reality than he ever imagined. Said he'd keep it to himself, so I told him about Parker. He was pretty upset, actually. Reality's awful sometimes."

"What about Nick?" A.J. said. "Can they get him for rape?"

"Statute of limitations," I said. "He gets away with it."

"Talked to anyone at Cherokee Point?" La Croix said.

I shook my head. "Don't want to either."

"Can't say as I blame you."

I looked at my watch. "Gotta go. Meeting Carmine at his office."

"At the hotel?" A.J. said.

"Yeah," I said. "Shouldn't be long. I'll walk back to the Cloghaun when I'm done." We'd decided to spend the night, take a bike ride, eat dinner, sit on the boardwalk and watch the sun set over the Mackinac Bridge.

"Okay," A.J. said. "Be careful."

I said to LaCroix, "You gonna follow me to the hotel?"

"No need," he said. "Notice anything when you got off the ferry this afternoon?"

"Not particularly," A.J. said.

"No Cicci or Rosato," I said. "Just you on the dock."

LaCroix nodded. "Carmine called 'em off."

"Nice to know," I said.

"Gotta learn to defend yourself better, Michael. You're gonna need it some time."

"Maybe you could teach some tricks you learned in Blackwater."

"Very funny," LaCroix said. "Aren't you late?"

I nodded and got up. "Have another drink," I said. "I'm off to see the Island's favorite crime boss."

57

I left Mary's and took Main Street east, towards the park. Hot, sunny weather always brought more people to the Island. The line to board ferries for the mainland reached the sidewalk. I went into the street to cut around the lines. Marquette Park was busy with people, adults and children, in no hurry to leave the Island or head back to their hotels.

I took one side of the curved driveway to the front door of the Marquette Park Hotel. I dodged suitcases and bags on the floor and made my way to the front desk.

"Can I help, sir," a Jamaican woman said from behind the counter. She was in her twenties and wore a blue blazer with the embroidered gold crest of the hotel on the breast pocket.

"Yes," I said. "Carmine DeMio is expecting me. Michael Russo."

The woman picked up a phone and punched a button. "Mr. Russo, sir." And hung up.

"This way, sir," she said and went to a short hallway off to the right. I followed. "The first door on the left. Knock first, sir."

I knocked and heard, "Come in."

I walked into a large square room with sash windows covering the wall opposite the door. Floor to ceiling bookcases lined the other three walls. A very large Oriental rug, mostly deep red, blue and green, covered all but a few inches of the floor. DeMio's desk, a large mahogany piece, sat just in front of the windows. Two chairs, also mahogany, sat in front of the desk. Off to the right was a fireplace with two small love seats facing each other with a coffee table in between. No fire today. Standing behind one love seat, next to the fireplace, was Joey DeMio. He wore black jeans and a peach V-neck sweater with a white T-shirt underneath.

"Hello, Mr. Russo." Carmine DeMio got out of his chair and came around the desk to shake my hand. Hadn't expected that. He wore, as before, a gray sharkskin suit over a black shirt and a black silk tie.

"Please sit down," he said, pointing to one of the chairs. Sure different than in my office. He threatened me, if I remember correctly. DeMio sat down behind his desk.

"Thank you for coming today," he said. "I wanted my son to be here, as well."

I looked over my shoulder and nodded. "Joey," I said.

Joey said nothing.

"Michael, there's a great deal that I could say. I obviously misjudged you. You said you were helping the police and I, well, let's just say I have reason to be suspicious of the police, so I didn't believe you. To make matters worse, when you said you could clear Joey of the murder charge, I didn't believe that either." He shook his head. "You were stubborn enough to ignore me when I urged you to leave us alone."

Is that what he calls a threat? An urge? And lawyers are accused of using jargon?

DeMio shook his head again. "You did exactly what you said you would do. Don't run into many people who do that, Michael."

Joey remained at the fireplace and still said nothing.

"Michael, did you believe from the start that Parker Abbott killed her father?"

I shook my head. "I had no one in mind right after the murder," I said. "Once Nickelson Abbott was cleared, I figured that Joey would be next in line."

"I told you that would happen," DeMio said. "Always happens when we're around, always will."

"You guys are easy targets," I said. "Not you two, in particular, but men in your line of work, shall we say."

DeMio chuckled. "Our line of work."

"Of course, you don't help yourselves sometimes," I said. "You can't come into a small community like Mackinac and let your men hassle the locals. I told you that before."

DeMio nodded. "I remember. That won't happen anymore," he said. "I've seen to that. You were right about that, too."

Two compliments in just a few minutes. More than I can take. "Thank you."

"So I don't forget," DeMio said, "Mr. Rosato and Mr. Cicci have other things to do than follow you."

"Thank you."

"I know you're here to have fun with Ms. Lester, so I won't take more of your time." DeMio leaned forward on the desk.

"I am in your debt for clearing my son of the murder charges," he said. "I owe that debt and I will repay your services."

I started to say something, but he cut me off.

"You may ask a favor. Whatever it is, whenever it is. If it is in my power to help you, I will. I owe you that."

"That's not necessary," I said.

"That is not for you to decide, Michael."

I did not know how to respond to that, so I said the first thing that came to mind. "A.J. and I would like two bikes. We want to ride around the Island this afternoon. How about we borrow them from your rentals?"

DeMio started to smile but caught himself. "That's not what I had in mind."

I shrugged. "What I need."

DeMio did smile at that one. His right hand touched something under the right corner of the desk. The office door opened and Carlo Vollini came in.

"Yes, sir?" Vollini said.

"Carlo, Mr. Russo needs two bicycles. Take care of that." He looked back at me. "Where are you staying?"

"The Cloghaun."

"Have them delivered to the Cloghaun Bed & Breakfast."

"Yes, sir," Vollini said.

"And Carlo?"

"Sir?"

"Two of the good ones. From the shed."

"Yes, sir," Vollini said and left.

"That's taken care of, Michael. You know, I could offer you much business. Legal business. We always have the need. It would be very lucrative. Is that of interest?"

Of interest? Sure, especially the lucrative part, but I read Nelson DeMille. I remember what happened to the lawyer in *The Gold Coast*.

"No, thank you," I said. "I like my struggling firm the way it is."

DeMio nodded. "When you need a favor." He stood and came around the desk. Meeting over.

One more thing," he said as we shook hands. "My son," he gestured at Joey, "has remained silent because this is difficult for him. He does not like to be in someone's debt. He wants to take care of things his way, on his terms. I wanted him to understand that this debt is mine, not his. I want you to understand that, too. Is that clear, Joey?"

Joey nodded.

"Michael?"

"It's clear."

"Well, then," DeMio said.

I nodded and turned to leave. Joey was examining the pattern in the Oriental rug. I stopped.

"Joey."

He looked up but not at me.

"I didn't do this to help you," I said. "You owe me nothing. I wanted to find out who killed Carleton Abbott. Simple as that." I opened the door and said, "Gentlemen. Have a good day."

58

I stopped on the front porch of the hotel. Two men and a woman, all in their sixties, sat in white Adirondack chairs, sipping iced tea and laughing. I took a deep breath and let it out slowly. I walked down the driveway to the sidewalk and turned towards downtown. In the marina, two Arnold Cats were leaving the dock for the mainland. Fifty feet away, I saw A.J. sitting on the low cement wall at the front of the park.

She smiled as I got closer. "Sit," she said, patting the top of the wall. I sat down.

"Warm in the sun."

"Summer in Northern Michigan," A.J. said. "We wait for this all winter."

"Yes, we do," I said. "Been here long?"

She shook her head. "Stopped at the bookstore for a few minutes. Then I tried to say hi to Fran Warren, but the shoe store was crazy busy. Waved and left. Came here."

I picked up A.J.'s hand and kissed it.

"You okay?"

"It's over," I said.

"Really?"

"Yep. Really."

We held hands and watched a steady stream of people go by on bikes. They mixed uncomfortably with taxis and a dray.

A wedding couple in a white carriage came down the street. The bride and groom smiled and waved to everyone who watched them. People waved back.

"How'd it go with DeMio?" A.J. said.

I told her.

"He's serious about the favor thing, isn't he?"

I nodded. "Don't imagine I'd ever call it in."

"You never know," A.J. said.

"Yeah," I said, "but it was important to him that I acknowledge it. So I did."

Two young teens tried to ride a tandem bike. They did not ride in a straight line. They were laughing. More out of fear than fun, I suspect.

"I made reservations at the Woods," A.J. said. "Michael's section in the back. Sound good?"

"Always sounds good. So does whitefish. Must be hungry."

"I'll call for a taxi," she said.

"Let's ride bikes," I said.

"We don't have bikes."

"Mon Cheri. We do have bikes." I told her the tale of two bicycles from the Marquette Park Hotel.

A.J. laughed. "Then we're ridin' bikes to dinner."

"Yes, we are," I said.

"Too bad DeMio won't accept the bikes as your favor."

"I tried that. Didn't work."

"Somebody oughta write a book," A.J. said.

"About all of it? Murder, mobsters, revenge, Cherokee Point?"

"Cherokee Point itself would fill a book," A.J. said. "Maybe Kelsey Sheridan would do it."

"Can't be him," I said. "Too inside. Knows too much. Be like Wall Street meets the Real Housewives of Harbor Springs."

A.J. laughed.

"The people at Cherokee Point are best left to themselves."

"Let's go investigator-man. We've got just enough time."

"To get our clothes off and jump in bed?"

She laughed again. "You have a one-track mind sometimes."

"Nice track," I said.

"Just enough time for a shower, Russo. We're goin' to the Woods."

ACKNOWLEDGEMENTS

I dreamed all this up, of course. That's part of the fun of writing fiction. Making it up. But several people helped make it more believable, clearer, and more readable. They include Frances Barger, Marietta Hamady, Stephen Hoffius, Charles Kleber, Wesley Maurer, Jr. Stephanie McGreevy, Aaron Stander, and Edward Wallon. The Mystery Writing Workshop at the Interlochen Center for the Arts, and the writers around the table, spiked my motivation again. What a delightful place to spend a few summer days. Fran didn't have to "hound" or "harass" me this time around, but she offered thoughtful and incisive critiques along the way.

Heather Shaw edited the manuscript. She deserves all the accolades I can toss her way. She turned my rough draft into a real book. The novel is the better for it, and she helps me be a better writer.

Peter Marabell grew up in metro Detroit, spending as much time as possible street-racing on Woodward Avenue in the 1950s or visiting the Straits of Mackinac. With a Ph.D. in History and Politics, Peter spent most of his professional career on the faculty at Michigan State University. He is the author of *Frederick Libby and the American Peace Movement*. His first novel, *More Than a Body*, was published in 2013. As a freelance writer, Peter worked in several professional fields including politics, the arts, and health care. In 2002, Peter moved permanently to Northern Michigan with his spouse and business partner, Frances Barger, to live, write and work at their businesses on Mackinac Island. All things considered, he would rather obsess about American politics, or Spartan basketball, after a good five-mile run on the hills of Mackinac Island.

Made in the USA
Charleston, SC
15 July 2014